Decoding 1

Dark Codes F

Marissa Farrar

CW01432014

Chapter One

Once more, I was under restraint in a vehicle, being taken to an unknown location.

Special Agent Lyle Hollan sat beside me, his gun held in his lap like an unspoken threat. In the front of the car, a second man called Stewart drove. He was the asshole who'd made a good show of copping a feel while he'd been giving me a pat-down. I intended to make sure he understood the repercussions of touching me without permission. A third man with red hair sat in the passenger seat, but I neither knew his name nor cared what it was.

An identical car followed close behind, this one containing two other men who'd helped to grab me in return for the freedom of my aunt.

"Where are you taking me?" I asked Hollan.

He looked at me from the side of his eyes. "You'll find out soon enough."

"How long is it going to take to get there?"

"Stop talking. I'm the one who should be asking the questions, not you." He jabbed the gun into my side. "Tell me what you're all doing way out here."

"We came to find my aunt."

"Yeah, I figured that much. But you were out here before then, weren't you? She wouldn't tell me where she'd come from, only that she was on foot."

1

A spark of hope ignited inside me. So, Aunt Sarah hadn't revealed the location of the base, as I'd feared she would. I wondered what had stopped her from doing so.

I shot him a glare. "We were driving, that's all."

"And your aunt happened to just hop out of the car and wander off?"

"She sneaked away while we were sleeping."

His eyes narrowed at me, and I forced myself to sullenly hold his gaze. He knew there was more to it, but there was no way in hell he was getting that information out of me.

Hollan sniffed and pulled a face, as though I was something gross he'd found on the bottom of his shoe, but he lowered the gun and sat back in his seat. I figured he thought he had plenty of time to run me through these questions, and that he had more persuasive ways of making me talk.

The cold metal of the handcuffs around my wrists dug into my skin. I tried to lean forward to prevent my bodyweight pressing against the back of the seat, causing the cuffs to feel even tighter, pressing into the small of my back. My shoulders ached from the angle they'd been yanked into, and no matter how much I tried to roll them to loosen up the joints, nothing made any difference to my discomfort.

Anger boiled and steamed inside me, puffing me up like a domestic cat—so I felt bigger than I actually was. Hollan might think he had won this by first taking my aunt hostage, and then exchanging her for me, but I was the one who was having the final laugh. Unbeknown to him, I had placed a tiny, skin-colored tracker behind my ear, hidden in my hairline. While he thought we were making a getaway, I knew this was all just a ploy to get him to lead us to where he was keeping the memory stick my father, Michael Sullivan, had died to protect.

My thoughts went to the men I hoped were following—Isaac, Kingsley, Clay, Alex, and Lorcan. What were they thinking of me now? Were they angry about what I'd done? I'd not discussed my plans with them beforehand for two reasons—mainly because it hadn't occurred to me until we'd been faced with him standing in the middle of the road, with his arm around Aunt Sarah's throat and a gun jammed to her head, but also because I knew they'd never have agreed to it.

Yeah, they'd be mad at me right now.

They'd be spitting blood and pissing fury.

Everything the guys had done since they'd come into my life had always been about protecting me. There was no way in hell they'd have supported me handing myself over to Hollan. Though they'd never have agreed to my plan, the fact they hadn't fought for me spoke volumes. I was sure some harsh words had been exchanged inside the van—that blond, rebellious Clay and serious, intense Lorcan, in particular, would have insisted on trying to take down Hollan on the road and set me free—but the leader of the group, Isaac, would have talked them down. And they listened to Isaac. He might not have agreed with my plan if I'd suggested it beforehand, but once it was in play, he knew it was the right thing to do.

Alex and Kingsley were the more nurturing of the group, and I imagined Alex making sure my aunt was all right, physically, while Kingsley, with his deep, soothing voice would be talking her down, and reassuring her I would be all right.

Now I just had to sit in this car, beside the man I hated most in the world, and let him take me right to the memory stick.

As the vehicle chewed up the miles, I tried not to think about the distance increasing between me and the guys, though I knew it had to be. Hollan had warned them that he would shoot me if he saw them trying to follow. They also wouldn't come after me with my aunt still in the van. They would need to take her somewhere safe—back to the base, I assumed. I also hadn't considered that they might not have the equipment with them to follow the tracker. Yes, Isaac always had his small but powerful laptop with him, but there was a chance the tracker needed to be followed using equipment from the base, or even that it needed to be switched on. Hell, I didn't know much about these things. I'd just listened to what their boss, Devlin, had told them about how discreet and powerful the tracker was, and I'd run with that.

A fresh flurry of nerves fluttered inside me. What if something had to be done to the tracker before it was placed onto someone in order for it to work? I hadn't considered that possibility. But no, I was sure Isaac would have said something when he'd had the opportunity. He'd watched me push the tracker into my skin and drop the empty box back into the van. But then I remembered him saying, "Darcy, no," as I'd left the van. Had he been trying to tell me my plan wouldn't work? Had I seriously messed up and handed myself straight into the hands of my enemy?

No, I couldn't let myself think like that. Devlin hadn't said anything about needing to do something to the tracker to get it to work when he'd been explaining it to Isaac and the others. This was anxiety and fear trying to creep into my brain. I needed to stay positive and strong. Hollan was going to try to get the code to unlock the memory stick from me, and I knew he was willing to use whatever tactics he needed. I had to stay positive that the guys knew my exact location and were coming to get me.

Before they reached me, however, I needed to make sure Hollan had revealed the location of the memory stick.

Hollan leaned forward, and I jumped at his sudden movement. He banged the back of the driver's headrest with his palm. "Pull over when you can. We're going to need to put the girl in the back. Can't have her seeing where we're going—not that I'm expecting her to ever be able to tell anyone."

His words sent ice particles coursing through my veins. He was talking about me not being able to tell anyone because his plan was to kill me. Of course, it was. He'd never allow me to walk free if he could help it. I knew far too much.

But yet, the worry must still be in the back of his mind that I would escape, or he wouldn't need to take such precautions.

The driver pulled over on the side of the road. This area was relatively free of traffic. Other than the car following us, which also belonged to Hollan, I hadn't seen another vehicle in some time. Wherever Hollan was keeping the memory stick, it was certainly a long way from Langley—not that I actually expected him to be keeping it there. Hollan and a handful of other corrupt agents were behind this, but there were plenty of other decent agents as well, like my dad. Hollan wouldn't have wanted to risk the chance of one of the good guys getting his hands on the memory stick again, so he moved it far away from where there was the possibility of that happening.

The car stopped, and the one following pulled in behind us.

Both men climbed out, and I remained seated, my arms still handcuffed behind my back. My heart thrummed in my chest, so fast it was hard to discern one beat from the next, and my breathing was shallow and quick. I forced myself to slow down, remembering Kingsley's deep and calm voice in my head—*breathe slowly in through your nose and out through your mouth.* My fingers felt cold and numb. The circles of the handcuffs were too tight around my wrists, but I knew complaining wasn't going to do any good. Chances were having too tight handcuffs was going to be the least of my problems.

The car door beside me opened with a clunk, and Stewart grabbed me, roughly pulling me out on the road. I caught the top of my head on the metal roof of the car, and I winced, my eyes filling with tears of pain. If either of the men noticed, they didn't care.

"Get her into the trunk," Hollan commanded. "She'll be less of an irritation in there, anyway. She's just like her father—asks too many damned questions."

Fresh anger rose inside me at the mention of my father. This was the man responsible for snatching my dad so brutally from my life. I would be a different person now if I hadn't gone through the trauma of having my father die in my arms when I was only fourteen. I could be one of those well balanced women who had a loving boyfriend and shared an apartment with her best friend. Maybe I'd even have a goddamned cat. Instead, I was making out with five guys at the same time, and spending half my life being kidnapped.

The trunk popped open, and I stared down into the empty space. I supposed I should be thankful I was getting it all to myself. It would have been just my luck if I'd had to share the trunk with a body or two Hollan had collected.

Stewart shoved me forward. "Get in there."

"It's not easy to climb into something when you don't have your hands free," I snapped.

"Fine." His tone was snide. "Let's give you a little help."

His hands left my arms and reached down to grab my hips. With a grunt, he lifted me and threw me over the edge. I managed to tuck myself in, but my body still slammed down on the hard surface, and I knocked the side of my head again. Panic that the movement might have dislodged the chip filled me. I wished I could lift my hand to feel that it was still in place, but of course, that was impossible. I told myself that was a good thing. I might check too often, and it would get noticed and make Hollan suspicious.

It would still be there. The tracker was the best ever made, Devlin had said. It wasn't going to fall out because of a little movement. They would have planned for that kind of thing.

I curled up on my side, my hands still wrenched behind my back, my cheek pressing against the cool floor of the trunk. Above me, Stewart and Hollan leaned over the gap, eclipsing the blue sky and the swaying branches of the trees above. I didn't want their faces to be the last thing I saw before the lid slammed down and I was shut in the dark, but I didn't want to squeeze my eyes shut either and put myself into premature darkness. I had no idea how long I would be in here, and I wanted to savor my final moments of light and fresh air.

"Make sure you behave yourself, Darcy," Hollan said. "If we pull over for any reason, and you start hollering your mouth off, I will shoot you through the back of the seat to shut you up. You understand? I won't even bother opening the trunk."

We both knew his threat was empty. He wouldn't kill me. Not until he'd gotten the code out of me. But then I wouldn't be making any noise if we were pulled over either. I didn't want to be rescued—at least not until Hollan had led me to the location of the memory stick.

I scowled up at him, but didn't bother to reply. Nothing I said would make any difference.

A slow smile spread across Hollan's face.

It was the last thing I saw as the trunk lid slammed down heavily above me, shutting me into darkness.

Chapter Two

I flinched as car doors slammed around me. I guessed Hollan had taken shotgun rather than sit in the back. He didn't need to since he'd dumped me in the trunk. I expected he'd have made the red-haired guy who'd been in the passenger seat take the rear, and I imagined the guy sitting with the barrel of his gun pressed against the backrest, ready to shoot me through it if I so much as made a sound.

The car engine roared to life, and then we were moving again. I bumped and jostled around in the back as we left the verge where we'd pulled over and got back on the road. I hated not having my hands free to be able to protect myself, to prevent banging my head again. A headache had started to form, a low throb that sank down through my brain and gathered behind my eyeballs. I suspected the headache had as much to do with stress as it did hitting my head.

How long would I be in here?

We'd already traveled for an hour or so with me sitting in the back seat with Hollan. Would we have about the same to go again? The thought of lying in this trunk for another hour, or possibly even longer, filled me with panic and dread, but there was nothing I could do about it. The smell of engine oil made me nauseated, and my mouth was so dry, my lips stuck to my teeth, and my tongue glued to the roof of my mouth. I'd barely managed to do so much as grab a drink of water that morning before realizing my aunt was missing, and all the adrenaline coursing through my body had sapped me of moisture.

Now no one could see me, I gave into the tears that had been threatening ever since I'd realized Aunt Sarah had gone. I cried silently, the salt tracking down my cheeks and soaking into the rough material of the floor of the trunk. I didn't want Hollan to know he had gotten to me, though I doubted he'd have heard me over the sound of the engine, but still I didn't give voice to my sobs.

My thoughts went to the guys. I needed to focus on them. They were my happy place. I thought of Isaac, and how surprised he'd been when I'd leaned in and kissed him. Had he wanted more of that? I'd always assumed from the way he acted with me—so cold and hard most of the time—that he wasn't interested in affection. But when I'd kissed him, he'd softened, if only for a fraction of a second, which was a miracle, considering the situation. What would happen if I got him alone and kissed him like that? Would he finally open up to me? Would I finally get to see Isaac's softer side? I hoped I'd live long enough to get the chance.

I pictured Lorcan, too, praying he was still coping with his injury. I wished I'd gone with my instinct to lay my head on his chest back in the medical bay, to have him put his arm around me while I listened to his heartbeat. Lorcan was another one who tried to come across as so tough, while I was sure he was soft as butter beneath all those tattoos.

I remembered how gorgeous Alex had looked in his white doctor's coat with his stethoscope draped around his throat, and of course, I couldn't help but think of the nights I'd spent with both Kingsley and Clay. Heat condensed between my thighs at the memory, and I pressed my legs together, feeling my inner muscles pulse in response. I hoped we'd all get a repeat performance soon, but right now I needed to be thinking about more important things than sex. Actually, screw it. I was handcuffed in the trunk of a car. I could think about sex if that was what got me through it.

And it did.

The car pulled to a halt, and the engine fell silent around me. I held my breath in anticipation, my ears straining for voices. Had we stopped because someone had pulled us over, and this was the point where I was supposed to keep quiet? Or had we stopped because we'd reached our location?

The crunch of footsteps rounded the side of the car. Every muscle in my body tensed, though I could barely feel my hands and fingers now. The lid opened, and I shied away from the bright light like a vampire, squinting, and trying to nestle deeper into the crevasse of the trunk.

The shapes above me were only black silhouettes while my eyes got used to the light. What time of day was it? It must be the afternoon by now, though I'd started to lose track.

The shapes began to distinguish into the growingly familiar faces of Hollan and Stewart, and the other man helping them.

"We're here," Hollan said. "Time to get up." He said it as though I'd been taking a nap, rather than having been locked in a trunk. "Lend a hand, Bryson." He jerked his head toward the third man. So it was Bryson. That was his name.

Both Stewart and the newly named Bryson moved into position. Bryson was shorter than Stewart, with the type of hair that was almost orange rather than red, and spattering of freckles across the bridge of his nose that made him look both younger and sweeter than I suspected he truly was. His eyes were green versus Stewart's muddy brown eyes, and at least they had a spark to them, whereas Stewart's appeared dull.

The two men reached for me, and I allowed them to grab me and pull me to sitting. I blinked back tears—these ones caused by the light rather than me feeling sorry for myself—and wished I could use my hand to wipe them away. Instead, I lifted my shoulder and wiped my tearstained, snotty face on my t-shirt.

I caught the glimpse of satisfaction—no, victory—on Hollan's face at my tears. That son of a bitch. This was a guy who'd known me as a child. Who'd watched me grow up, and had brought birthday and Christmas presents to my house. He'd also watched me holding my father as he'd bled out all over my lap. I shouldn't expect any kind of sympathy from him. He must have had his soul removed before his mother had given birth to him.

I also reminded myself what he was capable of, the reason he'd taken me and the memory stick in the first place. He wanted to put an end to places like the base where the guys had grown up. Was he really capable of killing the children who lived down there? Were the people he worked with capable of the same thing, too? It seemed too monstrous, even for Hollan. How many of those bases were dotted all over the country? Three? Five? Ten? Twenty? I had no idea. Would Hollan really try to wipe them all out if he was able to get his hands on their locations?

The two men hauled me out, my lower back and the rear of my legs banging and scraping against the edge of the trunk as they did so, and dumped me on my feet on the ground. My poor body had barely recovered from all the cuts and bruises it had sustained during the time back at the house, and now I was going to have to suffer a fresh round of injuries.

Bumps and bruises will be the least of your concerns after Hollan has had his way, a voice that sounded suspiciously like Aunt Sarah's said in my head. I thought of fingernails being pulled off with pliers, and a whole-body shudder shook me. I prayed Isaac and the others would reach me before anything like that happened.

"Come on." Hollan shoved me from behind. "We've got work to do."

As I was hustled forward, I quickly took in my surroundings. We were crossing a small parking lot that had seen better days. The asphalt was swollen and cracked, green tendrils of weeds pushing up through the fissures as though nature was trying to reclaim the place for her own. A building was positioned in the center of the space, a single story concrete structure consisting of squares that had all been shoved together, like a child's attempt at building a house out of Legos. Metal roll-down shutters covered the main entrance, large enough to drive a vehicle through, and almost every surface had spray-painted graffiti scrawled over it. Around the outside of the parking lot was a chain link fence that looked like it had seen better days, parts of it fallen and lying flat on the ground, as though it had simply given up.

The place looked abandoned from the outside, but one thing I'd learned over the past week was nothing was how it seemed.

I kept walking, though my legs felt weak and shaky. Hollan and the other guys were half holding me up, but I knew it wasn't done for my benefit.

Hollan reached the front of the building and then pulled something from a hook on his belt. It was a key fob. He hit the button, and the metal shutters started to roll up. "Bulletproof," he told me, and I picked up on the pride in his voice. "This whole place. Unless someone gets inside, they don't stand a chance of shooting their way in here."

His words caused acid to swirl in my gut. Was that his way of telling me it didn't matter if Isaac and the others found me—they had no way of getting in if they did. I hoped that wasn't true and they'd find a way.

The shutter stopped at a point barely high enough for us to get inside without having to duck. The second car had pulled up alongside the one I'd been taken from, and we waited for a moment for the two men to get out and join us.

With everyone inside, Hollan hit the button on the fob again, and the shutter began to roll back down.

"Welcome to my home, Darcy." Hollan gestured around him. "I'd say I hope you'll be most comfortable here, but we both know that isn't true."

"Fuck you," I spat.

"I'm afraid you're a little young for me, but I'm sure I have others here who will be happy to oblige."

I caught Stewart staring. I sensed how he looked at me, his gaze slipping down my body like oil, the look in his muddy-brown eyes telling me he wanted more. I prayed I wouldn't be left alone in a room with this asshole. I didn't know how far he would take things, and I didn't know how far I would have to go to protect myself. I wanted to glare at him, but the very real possibility of what he might be able to do to me struck home, and instead, my cheeks burned, and I felt hot and sick. I could handle a lot of things, but that?

I'd rather they tore off my fingernails.

Chapter Three

I didn't know what I'd been expecting from the place Hollan had brought me to. A house, maybe, like the one I'd first stayed at with the guys. Or a big military base. Not an abandoned building in the middle of nowhere. I'd been expecting teams of people bustling around, acting important, but instead, I was faced with a glass booth at the front of the building, which contained one guy wearing glasses manning the numerous security cameras, and, other than the men we'd entered with, that was about it. The interior of the building mirrored the outside in that it appeared industrial—concrete floors and block walls that no one had bothered to paint. Beyond the glass booth, the corridor led to both the left and right. The building itself was in the shape of a squared U, and we'd entered from the front.

I guessed the lack of personnel was because Hollan had to keep what he was doing quiet for the moment. He'd make up some kind of story to bring in the military once he'd gotten the location of the bases—not that I ever intended to allow that to happen.

Hollan turned to me. "Before all the ugliness starts, and you put me in a place where I have to force the number out of you, I don't suppose there's a chance you'll willingly give me the code your father put on the flash drive?"

I held his gaze. "Not a chance in hell. I know what you did. I know you killed my father. Nothing you can ever do to me will make me give up that code."

He paced, tapping his finger against his lips. "You know," he said lightly, as though reminiscing about happier times, "I wondered if you'd seen me the night your father died. It was part of the reason I started to put space between us after his death. At the funeral, I waited for you to say something, or give me any idea that you knew more than you were letting on, and yet you never did."

My lips pinched. "I didn't know there was anything to let on about. I didn't remember seeing your reflection, and at the time, I didn't know there was anything special about what my dad had told me as he'd died. I thought he was confused, mumbling nonsense." A thrill of bitterness went through me. "You know, if you'd only hung around long enough, you'd have heard the code for yourself as he told it to me."

He nodded. "I'm aware of that. Clearly something I regret not doing, but at the time I hadn't realized your father had encoded the memory stick. Had I known this, I might have been a little less quick to kill him."

Anger surged through me. "You'd have still killed him, though," I snarled.

He shrugged. "Of course. He knew far too much, just like you do now. I always took him as such a family man, and yet he gave you information that not only got him killed, but will now get you killed as well." His eyes narrowed. "I'm not sure he really thought it through properly."

"He was dying. I doubt he thought much through."

Hollan waved a hand dismissively. "Even so, it wasn't the nicest of things to bestow on your teenage daughter."

His words stabbed me, and I hated him for it, partly because it was the truth. But then Hollan didn't know about my synesthesia, and that that was the reason my father had told me what he had. He'd known I'd be able to visualize the number.

Hollan sighed. "Anyway, I assume all of this means we're going to have to do things the hard way?"

"Is the memory stick even here?"

He put his hands on his hips and turned to face me. "Now why would that be any of your concern, young lady?"

I jutted my chin defiantly. "Maybe I want to see the thing I'm most likely going to die for."

He waved a finger at me. "There's no need for that." He turned to a couple of his men. "Why don't you see our guest to her room?"

Stewart and Bryson grabbed me again, pushing and shoving me along the corridor to the right. Doors that looked like the entrances to prison cells, with hatches in the middle for passing things through, lined the walls. Though I'd chosen to be here, in a way, the sight of those doors filled me with terror. I hoped at any moment chaos would ensue as the guys arrived and proceeded to storm this place. I wasn't some damsel in distress, and I normally preferred to take care of myself, but right now I sure as hell could do with a little rescuing.

To my horror, we stopped at one of the doors and Stewart kicked it open. The interior was exactly as I'd pictured—a cell. Only prisoners would probably get better conditions. A thin mattress on a low, metal frame, foldout bed. A bucket to piss in. That was it.

What had I been expecting? Hollan planned to torture then kill me. It was hardly going to be a room in the Hilton.

Though this had been my plan all along, my fight or flight instincts set in. Things had been bad enough when I was locked in the trunk of the car; I couldn't let them lock me in this horrible little room.

My body seemed to act of its own accord, and I found myself pushing backward against the men, my heels pressing into the floor to prevent going any further forward. I shook my head, my shoulders shoving, trying to get the men away from me. I felt dizzy, lightheaded, as though I was no longer connected to the world.

"No, please. No."

Hollan's voice came from behind us. "Tell me the code, and you won't have to go in there."

If I told him the code, I'd be dead, and so would the boys back at the base, and however many more were out there.

Tears pricked my eyeballs, and I continued to shake my head. "No, I can't."

"Then you leave me with no other choice."

He stepped forward, and I thought he might hit me or threaten me with his gun again, then he pulled a small set of keys from his belt and worked the cuffs around my wrists. My arms sprang free, and I pulled them to the front of my body, giving a little cry of relief. My relief was short-lived.

A shove from behind sent me stumbling forward. I tripped over my own feet and landed heavily on the ground. My numb hands did little to break my fall, and I skidded across the rough concrete, face-first, grazing my cheek and skinning my palms. Behind me, the heavy door slammed shut, and a lock jammed into place.

Heavy footsteps walked away, fading as they went. Hollan obviously planned on letting me sweat it out a little before he started the interrogations. Good. That gave Isaac and the others more time to reach me before he started.

My face stung, and at first, I couldn't feel the wounds on my hands. I managed to push myself to sitting, the cold of the floor leaching through my jeans and into my backside. With my knees tucked up to my chest, I held my hands out in front of me. Tingles fizzed in the tips of my fingers as the blood flow increased, and tentatively, I squeezed my hands open and closed. The tingling spread, and with it came pain. Only it wasn't pain from where I'd skinned them, but instead my nerve endings firing off too quickly. I gave a cry and a whimper, wishing there was something I could do to help, but knowing there wasn't. My body needed to go through this in order for me to get the full use of my hands back.

I forced myself to flex my joints again, and tears of agony flooded my eyes. I willed the pain to be over, knowing I had to wait it out while wishing I could jump ahead in time. I clamped my teeth together, holding back any sound, not wanting to give Hollan the pleasure of hearing my pain. If he got his way, I suspected he'd be hearing a lot more of it, anyway.

Though it felt like forever, eventually the pain began to subside, and I was able to breathe again. I gave my fingers another couple of tentative tries—open and shut, open and shut—and though they felt fat and stiff, they were no longer agonizing. The grazes on my palms stung, as did the one on my face, but I'd survive.

Now that my body had released me from its torture, I was able to take a better look at my surroundings. I pushed myself back to standing and brushed down the seat of my jeans. A dim light was embedded in the ceiling—no chain or wire for a prisoner to hang themselves from—but it gave out no more than a muted glow, allowing me to see, but not in detail. From the door, to the flooring, to the walls, this place was a fortress of concrete and steel. There was no way out. I wasn't going to be escaping any time soon. The only items in the room were the metal foldout bed, with a thin mattress on top, and a bucket in the corner. I wrinkled my nose at the offending item. I assumed it was to be my toilet. A wicked thought that I'd throw whatever I did in there at Hollan went through my head, and, despite my circumstance, I allowed a bitter smile to crawl across my face.

No, I wouldn't be here long enough to need to use the goddamned bucket.

I lifted my hand and gingerly touched the spot behind my ear where I'd placed the tracker. My stomach lurched, my heart skipping, thinking I couldn't find it, but then my fingers grazed the tiny tracker, which lay almost flat against my skin.

The guys knew exactly where I was and were coming for me. They might be a few hours behind, due to having to get my aunt somewhere safe, and perhaps needing to plan or load up on more ammo—I didn't know for sure—but I knew they were coming. I had to hang onto that hope. If I didn't, I was as likely to die from a broken heart as I was at the hands of Hollan and his sidekicks.

The sparseness of the cell made me think back to the cellar the guys had kept me in when this whole thing started. I'd hated that place, had vowed never to go back down there, had raged and broken things, and slammed at the door demanding to be let out, but compared to this room, it had been a five star hotel. I'd had a big comfortable bed—which, stupidly, I'd refused to sleep in—plus a bathroom and changes of clothes. The guys had brought me meals, but I highly doubted I'd be brought anything here. If I were staying here for any length of time—which I wasn't—I expected Hollan would make sure I had enough water to keep me alive, but that would be about it.

On stiff legs, I walked around the edge of the room, counting my steps in barely a whisper. The numbers appeared in my personal space in front of me as I counted ...

"One, two, three, four, five, six ..."

The room was thirty-two paces around the edge in total, and as I thought this, the three and the two flashed in front of me.

With a sigh, I sank down on the edge of the bed and put my head in my hands. What the hell was I supposed to do now? Just sit here and wait? I'd never been good at sitting around doing nothing. Maybe it was my generation, but we always had something to distract ourselves with, and my brain didn't know how to function without it. I didn't want Hollan to come back, knowing it would mean he'd start asking about the code to the memory stick, and he would most likely use violence to get it, but at the same time, I hated the waiting.

It was a small comfort, but at least I didn't need to worry about my aunt's fears of not being able to trust Isaac and the others being true. Though my heart had screamed that she was wrong, I'd put a lot of weight on her opinion over the years, and, especially because of the way we'd all met, her words had haunted me.

Now I had no doubts Hollan was the bad guy.

Chapter Four

As I sat, waiting, I couldn't help but focus on each and every sound. Footsteps walking past the door. The metallic bang of doors slamming. The place felt and sounded like a prison, and I hated it. My main reason for listening, however, was in the hope I would hear something else happening, something that would signal the arrival of Isaac and the others. Would they be stealthy and sneak up on the place, or would they arrive with guns blazing?

That's if they're coming at all.

No, they were coming. They wouldn't just leave me, and, even if they did, which I was sure they wouldn't, they definitely wouldn't give up on the opportunity to get the memory stick back into Devlin's hands. They were tasked with making that happen, and right now I went hand in hand with that. But it wasn't only about the memory stick. They cared about me, and they wouldn't let me rot here, even if there wasn't the chance the stick was here as well.

They were happy to let you stay at the base after Devlin told them to leave without you.

These evil little ear worms, whispering negative thoughts into my head, trying to grind me down. Why was it the most negative influence in life was often that horrible thought in your own head?

I conjured up Kingsley's words, the ones he'd spoken to me right before we'd had sex. He'd told me I'd gotten under their skin, and they'd be crushed if anything happened to me. And I believed him. They wouldn't abandon me.

Lifting my hand to my mouth, I chewed at the dried skin around my nails, planning my next move.

I'd wanted to find out exactly where Hollan was keeping the memory stick before the guys arrived, but I couldn't do that locked inside here. I needed to get Hollan or one of the others to let me out.

With no sign of the guys arriving, I couldn't sit here any longer. If nothing else, I could at least try to get information out of Hollan about where he was keeping the memory stick. I loathed being in the man's presence, but once we got that memory stick back, I could take my ultimate revenge and kill the son of a bitch.

I got back to my feet and crossed over to the door. My body ached all over from being thrown around, but I ignored the pain. I stopped at the door. The hatch in the middle only opened from the outside, but I ducked my head and tried to see if there were any cracks I could look through. There was one right at the bottom, and I squinted, and then closed one eye, trying to get a view. The only thing I could see was the same corridor I'd been dragged down. It didn't look as though I had a guard stationed outside, or that anyone else was around. Even so, I balled up my right hand, wincing as I crushed the skinned flesh in the center of my palm, and then hammered my fist against the metal door.

"Hollan! Hey, Hollan! Are we doing this, or what?" I paused, listening for any sign I'd been heard, and then shouted again. "Come on, you sick son of a bitch. You've got me. Are you too frightened to ask me now? What are you scared of? That you'll never get the code out of me? That after all this time, I'll win, and my dad will have been the one to have the final laugh?" I hammered my fist again, not caring about the pain shooting daggers down through my arm. I was breathing hard, partly out of exertion, but mostly out of rage. I was frightened, too, of course, but my need to see Hollan pay overrode my fear.

The *cur-clunk* of a lock and door opening came from somewhere else in the building.

Footsteps, heavy, but hurried, headed toward me.

I took a breath and stepped back, my heart pounding. He was coming.

Ducking back down, I peered out of the crack in the hatch. Sure enough, in the tiny slit of light, Hollan walked toward me, still wearing the same suit he'd been wearing when he'd taken me from the road. The expression on his face read as 'seriously pissed,' and then he got too close for me to be able to see his face, the gray of his suit blocking my view as he came to a halt in front of the door.

"What are you doing, Darcy?"

I straightened. "I want to talk."

He barked laughter through the metal door between us. "Not about the code, I assume."

I didn't honor his question with an answer. "What are you going to do with me?"

"I think you already know that."

I shrugged, even though he couldn't see me. "So why aren't we getting on with it? Why just leave me locked up in here?"

"I'm waiting for a friend to arrive. He's the one who's going to get that number out of your head. He's extremely skilled at what he does, and I have no doubt he'll have you blurting out that number before long."

"Skilled?"

"Oh, yes. He's well practiced in getting people to talk."

I swallowed hard, trying to hold down the nausea swelling inside me. I knew what Hollan was saying—this man would torture me. I prayed Isaac and the others reached this place before he did.

"You don't like getting your hands dirty, then, Hollan?" I spat, trying to keep up my bravado. "Don't think you could do it yourself?"

"I'm quite capable of getting my hands dirty, young lady. Have you forgotten I was the one who shot your father? I'd considered killing you, too, when I realized you were also in the house, but I took mercy on you. Good thing I did, too, or the information on that memory stick would have been lost forever."

"Mercy on me? You left me with my father bleeding out on me!"

"It would have been just as easy to put a bullet in your head as well," he said, sounding perturbed, as though he couldn't understand why I wasn't grateful to him.

"So instead, you just left me with my dad dying in my arms. Maybe shooting me would have been the kinder thing to do?"

Maybe it would be better if that information was lost. I knew it wasn't what the guys wanted, and that it would mean the breakdown in everything they'd set up to beat corruption, but they'd functioned without it for the past six years. Couldn't they continue to function?

But they thought of each other as family. How I would feel if I'd been separated from my family, and then the only thing that would give me their locations was destroyed forever?

Hollan continued to talk to me through the closed and locked door. "Yes, but I still spared your life, Darcy. Maybe you should give me a little thanks."

I blinked in surprise, rearing back at the ludicrousness of his words. This man was insane. He'd killed my father and expected me to *thank* him for not killing me, too.

"You're crazy," I said lamely, bewildered by his response. Did he really believe he'd done me a favor?

We were getting off the point. My plan was to get him to reveal the location of the memory stick, not talk about what he'd done that night. I needed to focus on the future, not keep rehashing the past.

"Where is the memory stick?" I asked. "Is it even here?"

"Why would I tell you that?"

"You want something from me, so maybe you should give me something in return."

He chuckled. "I like your feistiness, Darcy, but really, you're the one being held prisoner. I don't think you have too much to bargain with."

"No? I think I have the most important thing to bargain with. I have the thing everyone wants."

"Don't think you can play tricks on me, young lady. When my associate gets here, we'll get the truth out of you, no matter what. There are drugs we can give you that will ensure you tell us what we need to know."

Alarm jarred through me. Drugs? I hadn't thought of that. I could hold out against them hurting me, but if they injected me with something that would make my tongue loose, they could make me spill my guts without ever laying a finger on me.

He must have noticed my silence, and he laughed. "Ah, now, that's got you worried. And you will tell me the truth. There's no point even attempting to lie to me after your veins are pumped full of this stuff. You'll have no option but to tell me everything."

I remembered how Kingsley had talked about how suggestible I was back when he'd been hypnotizing me, how he struggled to pull me back out of it after he'd put me under. Would it be even worse if I was given a drug that effectively did the same thing? Coldness coiled in my gut at the implication of that possibility. I could tell Hollan everything. I might even tell them about the base where the guys had grown up, and how many people were there, and how they had their guns taken from them as soon as they went inside, so they were all unarmed. I might tell Hollan everything I knew, including the code.

"Anyway," Hollan continued, "he'll be here soon, so how about you go and sit yourself down and stop making such a fuss."

I hate you. I hate you. I hate you. My thoughts were sharp and vicious, and I aimed them directly toward him, as though they could penetrate his heart and stop it from beating.

On the other side of the door, I heard Hollan's footsteps as he walked away again, leaving me to my thoughts. I was no closer to learning if the memory stick was even here.

Numb at the possibility of what might happen if this man arrived before Isaac and the others did, I slowly walked back to the bed. My legs felt weak, my stomach loose. Had I made a horrible mistake? I'd been stupid thinking hurting me would be the only method Hollan would have at getting the code from me. These people probably dealt with terrorists and people from other countries who'd compromised national security. How blasé of me to think some twenty-year-old girl from D.C. was going to last up against those kinds of methods. My legs crumpled, and I sat down heavily on the bed, trying not to hyperventilate.

I sent a thought out through the ether—*come on, guys. Please hurry up. I need you.* I knew they couldn't hear me, but that didn't stop me from wishing, like others would offer up prayers in times of need.

Chapter Five

The minutes passed by too slowly. I alternated between sitting on the bed, unable to bring myself to lie on it, and pacing around the cell, vocalizing my hatred of Hollan in fierce whispers, imaging all the horrible things I would do to him once I got the chance.

I was sitting on the edge of the bed when footsteps and voices approached once more. Jumping to my feet, I hurried to the door, then kneeled to peer through the crack in the hatch. Several men strode down the corridor toward my cell. One of them was Hollan, and the other two were his sidekicks, Stewart and Bryson. The fourth man I hadn't seen before.

He was tall—about six feet one—with hair so blond it was almost white, and eyes of the palest shade of blue I'd ever seen. I wondered if he was albino, but then I realized his skin was tan, so that wasn't possible. This was simply his coloring. Like the others, he was smartly dressed. I had a theory that men like them dressed in such a way to hide who they really were underneath. People were automatically suspicious of someone who dressed like Clay, in his baggy t-shirts and jeans, or someone like Lorcan, with his leather jacket and tattoos. Put a man in an expensive suit, however, and people automatically assumed they were decent, professional people, even if that was the furthest thing from the truth.

The new guy held a briefcase in his hand, and I fixated on it, my blood running cold. What was in that case?

As the men approached, their bodies blocked my view from the hatch. I scooted backward, wanting to put as much space as possible between me and them. I didn't think for a moment they were here for any good reason. I swallowed hard as fresh nerves danced in my stomach. Was this the man Hollan had brought here to deal with me? I'd hoped to have a little more time than this. Would they try to inject me here and now with the drug to make me talk? I had to figure out how to delay them and hope the guys would turn up at any moment. If they showed up, that would be enough of a distraction to stop Hollan's new colleague from injecting me, but for the moment, I was on my own.

The lock cracked back, then the door opened. I stood, rooted to one spot, trying not to tremble. I didn't want Hollan to see I was afraid, even though I was.

Hollan led the way, the new man at his side. His two goons lurked behind them in the doorway, ready to step in if I tried anything.

"Hello, Darcy," Hollan said with a cool smile. "I've brought someone to meet you."

"Well, I don't want to meet him," I snapped.

"Now, now. No need to be rude." He turned to the man at his side. "Obviously, this is the girl," he said, before focusing his attention back on me. "Otto needed to see you before getting to work. Apparently, it's important that he knows your size and weight."

I gave a bark of crazed laughter. "I'm not telling him what I weigh!"

It had nothing to do with modesty—my weight didn't bother me in the slightest—but I wasn't about to start giving him figures for him to use.

"It is no problem," said the blond. I detected an accent. "I can make an accurate estimation by looking at her."

I scowled and hunched over, trying to make it harder for him to guess my size. I remembered I was supposed to be delaying things. Maybe if I could get him talking, he'd see I was a real person, not some experiment to be injected.

"Where are you from?" I asked him, my eyes narrowed. "Russia?"

He laughed, revealing perfect white teeth. "No, I am from Sweden. But thank you for the stereotyping." His English was perfect, if a little stilted.

My nostrils flared, and I pressed my lips together. "Considering the circumstances, I don't think we exactly need to worry about being politically correct."

"No, I guess not." He held my gaze, a smile tweaking his lips. The bottom one was fuller than the top. He had good lips, I decided. I knew it was a ridiculous thing to be thinking about when I was about to be injected with some kind of concoction of drugs, but there wasn't a whole lot else to do. Besides, thinking he had good lips didn't mean I liked the guy. I hated the son of a bitch for what he wanted to do with me.

My gaze darted to the briefcase he still held. Did he have the drugs and equipment he planned on using on me in there?

"We are not doing it in here," he said, wrinkling his nose at the surroundings I'd been forced to inhabit. "I assume you have a better setting?" He looked to Hollan for an answer, who nodded in response.

"Of course. We have a medical room. I assume that would be preferable."

"Yes, that would be better."

The man—Otto—looked to me once more. "Do we need a chair with straps on the arms, or will you behave yourself?"

I spoke between gritted teeth. "I'll behave myself." I had no intention of doing anything of the sort, but he didn't need to know that.

He ducked his head in a slow bow. "Excellent. Shall we go through, then?"

Otto spoke like a man offering to take someone from the dining room into the study for drinks and a cigar after a good meal.

The two men who'd hauled me down here stepped forward and grabbed me by the arms. I yanked away from them. "I'm capable of walking."

They looked to Hollan, who shook his head. "No, keep hold of her. I don't trust her."

I scowled as the men held me tighter, their fingers digging into the skin and bone of my upper arms, pressing on the bruises they'd caused the last time they'd been dragging me around. Bastards.

Hollan and his new friend led the way, the briefcase swinging by his side. I was hauled along behind them. I was glad to be out of the horrible cell, but my mind spun at what was about to happen. The adrenaline coursing through my system made me dizzy and lightheaded, but I needed to focus and think clearly. Whatever happened, I couldn't let him inject me. I had no idea how I was going to stop it, especially with four big men around me, but I had no choice. I had to find a way.

They dragged me down a corridor identical to the one I'd been through when I was brought to my cell, but in the opposite direction, moving toward the back of the building instead of the front. In my head, I visualized what I'd seen of the outside of the building, trying to place myself within the blocky wings. I pictured that we were walking down the right-hand arm of the U-shaped building. How many ways were there in and out of this place? There was the main one, which we'd entered through, but I assumed there would be at least one at the back, as well. These kinds of places always had rear entrances. I knew my chance at escape was miniscule, but I also considered the possibility that the guys were already here, and were lining up outside, preparing to storm the place.

I knew I couldn't wait for help, however, even if it was right outside. By the time they found me, it would most likely be too late.

"Wait, please stop. I feel dizzy."

Stewart gave an uneasy glance from beside me. "What?"

"I feel really sick. I think I'm going to throw up." I allowed my legs to go loose beneath me, so both men had to hold me up. The way I slumped made them lean over me. I thought of the most revolting thing I'd experienced—finding a half formed baby chick inside a boiled egg

I'd been eating when I was a child—and started to gag. My stomach crawled up my throat and I retched, the sound coming from my throat, rasping through the otherwise silent corridor.

"Ah, fuck." Bryson dropped his hold on me and stepped away. I was dangling from Stewart's grip now, but I felt it had loosened, his revulsion taking hold. I twisted slightly and retched again, this time making sure I was pointed directly at his feet. Though there was nothing in my stomach to come up, he still gave a cry of disgust and jerked away.

I took my moment. With a burst of energy, I straightened and took off at a sprint, back in the direction we'd come. Cries of surprise and annoyance followed me.

"Get after her!" Hollan's angry shout.

I ran, my feet pounding the solid concrete floor. I didn't hold any hope of finding an exit I could escape from, but this was about me buying time for the guys to arrive, not me trying to escape. I needed to find somewhere I could hide, but I knew Hollan would know the layout of this place better than I could ever hope to. My chances of finding anywhere for long were minute, but that didn't stop me trying.

I passed the cell I'd been kept in and veered off to the right. The area where I'd first been brought in was at the end of this corridor, and, though there was an exit, I hadn't seen anything that would be a good hiding spot. No, I was better off taking my chances and hoping to find something different.

Behind me, the sound of feet running met my ears. The men were taller than I was, with longer strides, and most likely faster, but I'd had the advantage of a head start. I passed the entrance with its glass booth, though the man inside only watched me run past, his expression a startled surprise. I kept going to the end, before veering off to the right and running down the second arm of the U-shaped building. Did Hollan have a phone on him? How many people were in this building? I'd arrived with four men, plus I'd seen the guy in the booth, and then there was the big Swede. I didn't know if any of the men I'd arrived with had left again, but there was a good chance they were still here somewhere. The place was big enough for me not to have seen them since we'd first gotten here. Was Hollan calling for backup, and I'd find myself surrounded?

Other doors led off the corridor, but they weren't the metal cell doors of the parallel corridor I'd been kept down. They were glass and wood, regular doors. Panicked, my heart racing, I grabbed for the handle of one and twisted. To my astonishment and relief, the door swung open, revealing a dark interior. I threw myself inside and grappled for the door to slam it shut behind me. I let out a sob of relief as my fingers touched a key inside the lock, and, holding the door shut with my shoulder, I was able to turn it and the lock clicked into place.

The sob escaped my mouth, and I fell away from the door, scrambling backward. They'd seen me come in here, I was sure. They hadn't been that far behind. But then footsteps ran past. I heard shouts of 'where'd she go?' and 'Darcy?' as though I'd actually answer.

I huddled into a ball, my arms wrapped around my legs. My entire body shook from fear and exertion as I stared wide-eyed at the door. They'd find me quickly enough, but I'd managed to do more than I'd hoped for, and had bought myself some time.

Chapter Six

What sort of room had I found myself in?

I wondered if there might be something in here that could help me.

I tore my attention from the door and looked around, blinking, willing my eyes to get used to the dim light which filtered in through the windows onto the corridor. Half-open blinds prevented anyone from looking directly in, but it also shut out the light from the corridor. I didn't want to find a switch on the wall, knowing turning it on would be a beacon to my location.

Gradually, my eyes got used to the gloom, and I was able to make out more of the room I'd hidden in. I was in an office with the usual set-up—a desk, a chair, a filing cabinet. Uninspiring pictures of cityscapes in black frames hung on the walls, and a faded rug covered the floor. None of that would be of any use to me, and my gaze darted back to the desk. Of course, there was a computer with an older style monitor, and a phone. A phone!

I'd never been given the cell phone number of any of the guys, but I still knew my aunt's number. But had she still had her bag when we'd found her on the road with Hollan? I tried to picture the scene in my mind. No, she hadn't had it on her person, but I was sure I'd seen it thrown to one side, discarded. Would she have insisted on picking it back up after Hollan had taken me, or had she been too distressed and had left everything on the side of the road? That didn't sound like my aunt at all, but these weren't normal circumstances. I guessed the only way I'd find out was if I tried the number. If the guys had taken her back to base, and she was deep underground, the phone wouldn't work anyway. But still, it was worth a shot. I had no idea what I would say to her, how she could help, other than getting Devlin to tell the guys to hurry the fuck up, but still I had to try.

I snatched up the phone and pressed it to my ear. It had a dial tone, thank God.

Anxiously, I glanced back toward the door. The footsteps and voices had gone past me, but now they were getting louder again, coming closer. I heard the sound of doors opening and shutting, my name being called. They'd figured out I'd darted into one of the rooms. As soon as they tried this door and found it locked, they'd know exactly which one I'd run into.

As I recalled my aunt's phone number, the digits appeared in my vision. Four ... One ... Five ... Five ...

I took comfort in seeing the numbers appear, as though they were old friends, instead of the thing that had gotten me into all this trouble.

I punched in her number as it appeared around my head. I willed for the phone to ring, but instead it went straight through to voicemail.

"You've reached Sarah. Please leave me a message, and I'll get back to you as soon as I can ..."

At hearing her voice, I barked out a sob of despair, and then pressed my fist to my mouth to hold back the sound.

I pulled myself together enough to speak and left her a message. "It's Darcy," I managed to croak, willing my voice not to crack. "You have to tell the guys to hurry. Hollan's trying to inject me with something that will make me tell him the code, and everything else I know. Please. They need to hurry!"

The door handle turned, and I froze, staring at the shapes on the outside of the door. The top panel was privacy glass, but I was still able to see through it. They were here.

"It's locked," a male voice said.

A different voice came next. "She's in there."

Shit.

I dropped the phone and looked for something I could use as a weapon. Perhaps I should have done this before I'd tried to make the phone call, but it was too late to think of that now. Everything on the desk was useless—a pot of pens, a calculator, a charger for a phone. Frantic, I yanked open the drawers and rifled through the paperwork I found there. My fingers closed around cool metal. *Yes!* It was a pair of scissors—not huge, but big enough to cause some damage when stabbed into a throat or eye.

"Open the door, Darcy!" I recognized Hollan's voice. "We know you're in there. Don't make me shoot my way in. You know I'm more than capable, but to be frank, I'd rather not make a mess of my woodwork."

Fuck his woodwork. He could shoot the whole place down, for all I cared.

But something he said pinged inside my head, and I realized I was brandishing a pair of scissors against several armed men. The moment they saw the blades, they'd point a gun at me and pluck them out of my hand. No, I needed to be smarter than that. I needed to pick my right moment, and it wasn't now.

I still wasn't opening the fucking door, though.

I stared down at the scissors in my hand and tried to figure out what the hell to do with them. I didn't have time to think of anything smart, so I just shoved them down the side of my bra, hoping the elastic would hold them in place against my ribs, and that I didn't manage to slice off a breast while they were there.

Crashing came at the door, the panel bowing inward. Remembering my need to buy time, I got behind the desk, putting something between us. Damn, I should have moved the filing cabinet over, too, but it was probably too heavy for me to move, and I hadn't had time to think of it.

The door burst inward, flying open. The four men filled the gap.

I wanted a break, just to be able to put both hands up and call for a time out, but I couldn't give up. I'd keep fighting for as long as I had to.

"Get her," said Hollan to the two men who'd let me go, jerking his head toward me. "And try to keep a better hold this time."

I took some pleasure in knowing I'd fooled them, if only for a few moments.

The two men stalked toward me, Stewart leading the way, his muddy brown eyes narrowing in a scowl. Bryson followed, his arms held out in a circle as though I was a farmyard animal they were trying to round up. Stewart, however, stalked forward with his gun held at his side, though I didn't think he'd shoot me. Hollan would be pissed if he did.

I waited until he got close enough, then put my hands on the computer screen and gave it a shove. Being an older style, it was heavy, and toppled off the desk and smashed at his feet, the screen exploding into a thousand pieces.

"Crazy bitch!" he swore.

Bryson darted toward me, but all I had left was the phone, so I threw that at him. It bounced harmlessly off his shoulder, and then he was on me, his arm wrapped around my chest, pinning me against him. I struggled, trying to get in a jab of an elbow, or to kick his shins, but he held me too tight.

Stewart flashed his gun at me. "Calm down, bitch. We're not allowed to kill you, but no one said anything about a bullet in the hand or foot." That threat was enough to make me fall still. I didn't want to give them an excuse to shoot me, even if it wasn't going to be life threatening.

"Right," said Hollan, exasperated, his hands on his hips. "Let's try that again, shall we?"

The new arrival, Otto, lurked behind him.

I wondered who all these men worked for on a day-to-day basis. Were they government men like Hollan, or were they individual agents who hired out their services? If so, what did they make of situations like this, or did they think it wasn't their business to care? They were being paid to do a job, and that was all. What went on behind the scenes was none of their concern.

They hustled me back out of the room, through the busted door. I kept my arms pinned to my sides the best I could, so the men didn't accidentally brush the scissors still stuffed down the side of my bra. I had a weapon, but I'd much rather have Isaac and the others arrive sooner than later. I didn't know how much longer I'd be able to hold out.

I wanted to keep fighting, but my last sprint for freedom had left me exhausted. The briefcase was still in the Swedish guy's hand, and I knew they were taking me back to the room to inject me with the drugs. Desperation filled me. I couldn't let it happen, but I was all out of options. There was no way they'd let me run again now.

Feeling helpless and bleak, I resorted to begging. "No, please. I'm too tired now. Just let me rest for an hour, and then we can do this." I struggled against Stewart and Bryson, but my limbs were heavy with exhaustion, and my efforts felt futile.

Hollan laughed. "You can't think I'd give you anything you asked for after that performance? No, young lady. This is going my way now."

My sole focus was on trying to delay things, but I felt as though I was all out of options.

"Can I have some water?" My throat was painfully dry after the running and adrenaline. Yes, I was trying to postpone things, but I was also desperate for a drink. My lips glued themselves to my teeth, and my tongue felt like a fat, furry slug pressed against the roof of my mouth.

He glared at me as though I'd asked for champagne. "No, you fucking can't."

The four of us continued to move down the corridor like one entity, but we were interrupted by someone walking toward us.

The younger man in glasses, who'd been manning the security booth at the front, approached. Behind the black frames, his eyes darted anxiously between us. "Umm, sorry to interrupt, sir, but you have a phone call."

Hollan drew to a halt. "Can't you see I'm busy?"

The man pulled himself straighter, putting his shoulders back. "It's important, sir. I wouldn't have interrupted otherwise."

I wondered what had happened to the two men who'd arrived with us in the second car. Were they still in the building, or had they been sent off to do other things?

Hollan gave a huff of exasperation. "God dammit. Okay, fine. Put her back in the cell. I guess this will have to wait."

My heart lifted. It wasn't anything I'd contributed to, but it looked like I was getting some extra time after all.

Hollan must have sensed my relief, as he narrowed his eyes at me and growled. "You got your rest, but it won't be for long, got it?"

I nodded, not speaking. I didn't want to say anything that might make him change his mind.

Chapter Seven

I never thought I would be happy to be locked back up in this hideous room, but the relief of it caused my entire body to sag and I gulped back tears. The door slammed shut with a metallic clang, and the lock cracked back into place.

Exhaustion from my fight, combined with the adrenaline rush leaving my body, left me shaky. I staggered to the poor excuse for a bed and sank down onto the edge. I leaned forward and put my head in my hands, trying not to hyperventilate. That had been close. Had I not managed to run and lock myself in the room, I'd have found myself pumped full of some kind of drugs and most probably spilling my guts right now. My thoughts raced. What was it they used in the movies? I was sure I knew the name. Truth serum? No, there was a more technical name than that. It came to me. Sodium pentothal. That might be what they'd try to inject my veins full of, and I already knew I was suggestible from Kingsley hypnotizing me, so I didn't doubt for a moment that I'd tell Hollan everything I knew. Dammit. I thought back to my time in the cellar. When Kingsley had told me I was suggestible, it had felt like an insult. Now I understood why. It was a weakness, and I had no control over it.

But if I wasn't suggestible, I might never have recovered those memories. I might never have remembered I'd seen Hollan the night my father died, and that he was responsible for killing him. I might still be in the dark.

I tried to swallow against my bone dry throat. All the running, combined with the adrenaline and not having had so much as coffee that morning left me parched. I knew Hollan wouldn't take any pity on me. In desperation, I did a quick search of my little cell, hoping I might have missed something, and maybe someone who'd been kept here before me had left a half drunk bottle of water beneath the bed, but there was nothing. Apart from the bed and the bucket, the room was empty.

Despondent, and with little else to do, I dropped back down on the bed. I wanted to lie down, but I didn't like the idea of pressing my body against the dirty mattress. I didn't know who'd been here before me, and the thought of possible sweat, blood, and tears made me shiver with revulsion. I hoped I wouldn't be here long enough to warrant sleeping. The way things were looking, even if the guys didn't arrive to rescue me, Hollan would get what he wanted and kill me anyway.

I pressed my fingers to the side of my ribcage, where I had the scissors held in place by the strap of my bra. At least I had a weapon. It wasn't much of one against a gun, but I'd use it if I had to. I remembered the razorblade I'd gotten hold of back in the cellar, and how I'd slashed at Isaac's arm. I wouldn't make the same mistake again. While now I was glad I hadn't gone for Isaac's throat or eye, nothing would stop me from stabbing Hollan in the right places, if I got the chance.

I wondered what had been the cause of the phone call. Dared I hope it had something to do with the guys, and that they were coming here for me? I didn't want to get my hopes up, but I couldn't help it. I wished I'd worked out where Hollan kept the memory stick by now. When the guys arrived, I wanted to be able to tell them exactly where it was, and I wanted to be able to reassure them I hadn't said a word. This was my dream ending, of course, my fantasy world. In that world, I also managed to shoot Hollan in his psychotic fucking head, but like I said, this was a fantasy. I also clutched to the hope that the guys would let me stay with them when all this was over, instead of sending me back to my old life, but now that I'd met Devlin, and seen what sort of lives they lived, I wasn't sure that would be possible, even if it was what everyone wanted.

Dark thoughts plucked at my brain. What if they weren't coming? What if the tracker wasn't working? It might be faulty, and Isaac and Kingsley and the others had no idea where I was. Were they cursing me for being reckless and stupid once again? No, my plan was a good one. It wouldn't have been my fault if the tracker wasn't working. That would be down to Devlin for providing Isaac with faulty equipment.

I couldn't let myself think that way. The tracker was fine, but the men would have needed to regroup and plan. They wouldn't rush into this without figuring out exactly what was going on first. They'd check the layout of the place and work out what they needed to do to get me out. Plus, they'd had Aunt Sarah with them, and they wouldn't have wanted to bring her with them.

I hoped Sarah wasn't blaming herself too much for what had happened. I knew she would a little—how could she not? She must have contacted Hollan herself, unless he'd put some kind of tracker in her phone, which was also a possibility. But at the end of the day, she'd left without telling any of us, and that was what had put her at risk, together with not believing me when I'd told her the truth about Hollan being the one who'd killed my dad. It was a small comfort, but at least she had to believe me now. I hoped we'd get the chance to reconcile. I hoped I wouldn't die in here, with her blaming herself.

I also couldn't help but think Devlin and even Isaac were also somewhat to blame. They'd put what my aunt had done back on me, but perhaps they needed to ask some questions of themselves and their own security. Yes, they'd said they'd trusted me and my aunt because of our link to my father, but they should have done more, too. They should have searched her bag, or put extra security on her. Maybe their security was lax because the place was a home more than a prison, but they'd still failed in their own way.

A gentle knock came, and I sat up straight, staring at the door. My heartrate jumped. Who the hell would be knocking? It wasn't as though I could open the damned thing anyway.

The lock clicked open, and I jumped to my feet, preparing myself for fight or flight. Was there a chance it was one of the guys? Was Hollan dealing with them now, and that was why he'd left me, but one of them had gotten past him?

The door cracked open, and my heart swelled with hope. Then it burst again as the tall Swedish man with the icy blond hair and pale blue eyes stepped through the gap.

I froze, my whole body tensing. What had Hollan called him? Otto?

He moved into the cell, and I took a step back, keeping the distance between us.

"What do you want?" I demanded.

He held something out between us, and my gaze flicked down to the object. A pulse of need pounded through me, and I stepped forward, though I'd had no rational thought in doing so. My body did what it needed.

I reached out to the bottle of water Otto held in his hand. It was exactly how I'd been imagining one to be—fresh, and new, and chilled, the condensation pricking beads to the sides of the bottle.

"Quickly," he said, waving it at me. "He does not know I have brought it to you."

We both knew who he meant when he said 'he.' Hollan.

He held the bottle out to me as one might offer a piece of meat to a wild animal. I was more afraid of him than he was of me. I darted forward and snatched the bottle from his hand, quickly cracked open the lid, then placed the bottle to my lips. Cold water flowed over my tongue, and I gulped gratefully, feeling the liquid soothe my sore throat and settle in my belly.

I'd almost drained the bottle, but forced myself to save some. I screwed the lid back on, and, with nowhere else to hide it, pushed the bottle beneath the thin mattress. The bulge of the bottle looked obvious to me, but I was looking for it. Hopefully Hollan wouldn't notice in the dim light.

I turned back to Otto, who remained lurking in the doorway. I assumed Hollan was preoccupied somewhere else in the building.

"Thank you. You didn't need to do that."

He shrugged. "It did not seem right to deny you of a basic need like water."

"Or freedom?" I said, gesturing at my surroundings.

"You can live without freedom," he replied.

"Not for long."

He stared at me, and I wondered what he was thinking.

"What has Hollan told you about me?" I asked, being the one to break the silence.

"That you are holding back information of national importance."

"Did he tell you why?"

He shook his head. "It is not my job to know why."

"Your job is to get information out of people's heads."

He pressed his lips together. "My job is to get the truth."

"Hollan killed my father—an FBI agent. How's that for the truth?" I watched his face, seeing if my words had any impact. He was either really good at hiding it, or they simply had no effect.

"Your father betrayed your country and stole material of national security. According to Hollan, you and your father are very much alike."

So Hollan had gone with that story. Of course this man was going to believe him. I hadn't been able to get my own aunt to believe my version of events, so I stood little chance of getting this stranger to take my side.

I shook my head, sudden sadness sweeping over me. "Believe what you want. Nothing I say is going to make any difference. But thank you for the water, I appreciate it."

He ducked his head in a nod. "You are welcome."

"Oh," I added, as though I'd forgotten something, "and you know Hollan is going to kill me, too, as soon as you've gotten that information from me. I just thought you should know."

A cloud passed across his clear features. Yes, that part had gotten to him. He hadn't considered that Hollan would kill me. What had Hollan told him? That I would be prosecuted and serve my time in jail? I guessed Hollan killing my father was palatable because he'd been a grown man, but the idea of murdering young women sat less easily on Otto's shoulders.

Noise came from somewhere else in the building, snatching our attention.

Without saying another word, he glanced over his shoulder. Quickly, he backed away and pulled the door shut, locking it into place. He clearly didn't want to be caught fraternizing with the enemy.

I let out a sigh and sat back down on the bed.

I felt better now that I'd had a drink, but nothing about my situation had changed. Hollan would come for me soon, then I'd have to fight again.

If the opportunity arose, I'd stab Hollan with the scissors, but first I needed to find out what he'd done with the memory stick.

Chapter Eight

I thought perhaps an hour or so had passed since Otto brought me the bottle of water, though I couldn't be sure. My hopes that whatever Hollan had been called away to deal with was to do with the guys arriving started to fade. Something else would have happened by now. I'd have heard Hollan calling his men to mobilize, or gunshots would have sounded from outside as Isaac and the others tried to storm the place. Instead, there was nothing more than a frustrating silence. There hadn't been so much as footsteps passing by my door.

I agonized over what the guys were doing. Where were they? Had they given up on me? Did they not know my location? I put my fingers to the tiny tracker. *Are you even working, you piece of shit?* I hissed at it mentally. I wished there was some way of knowing. All the wondering was driving me crazy.

To keep myself busy, I got back to my feet and did another round of the cell, running my fingers across the brick walls. I scraped my feet across the concrete floor, hoping in vain that I might have missed something the first time. On my hands and knees, I found a brick near the bottom of the far wall that was looser than the others. Could something be hidden there? I scraped and worked at the mortar surrounding it, digging my nails in to work chunks loose. It was partly something to do, but also in this crazy world I'd found myself thrown into, it wouldn't have surprised me in the slightest if some pervious prisoner had hidden something for the next unfortunate soul to find. I scraped my fingertips over and over at the surrounding mortar, each dribble of dust I managed to dislodge sending my heart racing a little more. I was hanging on to a stupid hope, a fantasy, but as the minutes passed, and the crumbling mortar only revealed more solid brickwork behind, I realized I was expending my energy for nothing.

I slammed the heels of my hand against the brickwork. "Stupid, mother-fucking piece of shit!"

Sitting back on my heels, I felt insanely angry at a wall that had done nothing except refuse to be anything more than just a wall. The pads of my fingers were red and raw from all the scraping they'd done, and now the moment was fading, they were starting to sting.

I was losing my goddamned mind.

I rubbed my hands over my face, exhaling a heavy sigh. Behind me, the door clicked open. I snapped out of my stupor and jumped back to my feet, spinning to face it.

Hollan's hateful figure stood in the doorway. "Ready for round two, Darcy?"

I scowled at him. "No."

"You won't be running this time. Do you understand me? The moment you show any sign of trying to escape, I will make sure one of my men puts a bullet in your leg."

How much did it hurt to get shot? I remembered Lorcan's pained expression. A lot. If someone like Lorcan had struggled, I'd be a mess. But it was better to get shot than give over the code. The idea filled me with horror, but what else could I do? He wouldn't kill me. That was what I needed to hang onto. As long as he didn't have the code, he needed to keep me alive. And I need to stop Otto injecting me with the sodium pentothal, if that was even what he was using. Even if it meant getting shot.

"What was the phone call about?" I asked, changing the direction of the conversation, hoping to delay things.

"Nothing for you to be concerned about."

Had someone called in a warning? A sign that the guys were somewhere around, closing in on this place? I was clinging onto hope by my fingernails, but I didn't have any choice. They were what was stopping me giving up, and the thought that they might be somewhere nearby caused my determination to solidify inside me.

"Right," he said, "Let's get on with this."

He jerked his head, and, at his unspoken command, Stewart and the other guy, Bryson, stepped forward. I prayed they wouldn't think to handcuff me again. If they did, the pair of scissors I had shoved down the side of my bra would be useless. I couldn't use them as a weapon if I couldn't reach them. But it was tantamount to the cockiness of Hollan and the other men that they thought even if I was able to run in this place, I'd never get anywhere. They just saw me as a weak woman, not an adversary against four fully grown men, with probably more in the building. I hoped I'd get the chance to prove them wrong.

As they stepped into the room, I took several paces backward. I didn't want to make any part of this easy for them. I hated the thought of Stewart's hands on me—the man made my skin crawl. I wasn't going to fight them physically, not yet, because I didn't want to give them an excuse to handcuff me, or tie me up in any way, but I still wasn't going to go easily.

I darted to the back of the cell, wishing I had something to put between us. I could have pushed the bed across the floor toward them—it was lightweight enough—but I was horribly conscious of the bottle of water I'd hidden beneath the mattress. I didn't want it to roll out, partly because I thought I might need the water, but also because I didn't want to have to explain how the bottle got there. Otto was my enemy right now, but that small act of kindness told me he might became an ally, if I played things right.

Moving to the back of the cell bought me mere seconds. With a couple of long strides, Steward was on me again, grabbing me by the arms. Bryson stepped in to help, so they held me between them and yanked me back to the front of the cell again. Hollan and Otto remained in the open doorway, watching events go down. I glared at Hollan, though I knew it would make no difference. Otto once again held the briefcase, which I assumed contained everything he needed to inject me with this drug, at his side.

Both men stepped out of the way as I was dragged back into the corridor.

I looked to Otto, standing to one side, pleading to him with my eyes. I knew he had a heart inside that ice cold exterior. He wouldn't have brought me the bottle of water if he didn't care in the slightest about my welfare.

"Please," I begged him. "You don't have to do this. Just say no. They can't force you to do this to me."

Otto's expression showed no emotion. His accent made his voice stilted. "I am sorry, but I am a professional, and I have been paid to do a job."

"Everything he's told you is twisted. There are people's lives at stake—children's lives. If you do this, their blood will be on your hands. I hope you can live with that!"

Stewart gave me a rough shake, rattling my teeth. "Shut it, you."

But I wasn't going to be silenced so easily. "I'm one of the good guys. I'm trying to protect people. Hollan is the one who's betrayed his country."

I didn't think my words would make any difference. I had already told him Hollan had killed my father, and he was still here, determined to inject me with the drugs that would make me spill the truth. I guessed he'd been in this position countless times before, where someone he needed to work on claimed the other person was lying. It wasn't his job to play judge and jury. It was his job to do what he was paid to do.

The men hauled me back down the corridor, passing the place where I'd stopped to pretend to throw up only an hour or so ago. I knew I wouldn't get away with playing the same trick twice. I stared around as I was dragged, hoping to see something or someone who might help me. The thought of Hollan getting the code out of me filled me with both dread and a horrific sense of failure. I'd sworn I would never give the number up, yet now I was facing the very real possibility I would do exactly that. I'd be the one responsible for getting all those people and children killed. The idea of the boys I'd seen—the red-haired boy who'd blushed when I'd smiled at him—lying slaughtered in the underground bunker they called a base, filled me with horror. Dead was dead, and if that happened, there would be no turning the clock back or making things right.

We stopped outside a door at the end of the corridor. Hollan led the way, opening the door and standing to one side, allowing Stewart and Bryson to push me through.

Otto followed behind, his case held firmly in his hand.

I found myself in a medical bay, similar to the one Lorcan had been in back at the base. There were a couple of beds divided by curtains that were currently pulled back, but could be pulled into place to offer privacy via the runners attached to the ceiling. There was also a separate room divided by glass, with shutters on the outside of the windows to block out prying eyes, but again, they were currently open. In the center of the glass room was an operating table. Numerous stainless steel trolleys and other equipment were positioned around the outskirts of the room. Hollan must have this here in case one of his men was shot or hurt. I guessed he wouldn't want to take him to a regular hospital, especially not with a gunshot wound, and be put in the difficult position of explaining what had happened. Considering how Hollan went about his business, I guessed he wouldn't want any of the other authorities to start asking questions.

"What do you need?" Hollan asked Otto.

Otto nodded over to one of the beds. "Do those go into an upright position?"

Hollan nodded. "Yes, close enough."

He crossed the room to the nearest bed and found a lead with a switch on the end of it. He pressed one of the buttons, and a whirring came from the mechanism. The top third of the bed began to rise, the bottom third dropping down, to bring the bed into a more chair-like position. This was where they planned on having me seated while they pumped my veins full of shit.

I pulled back on the men holding me, but they pushed me forward, shoving me into the seat. They were strong, and Stewart moved behind the chair, so he could hold me by the shoulders, keeping me pinned. My heart raced, and I gasped for breath. This was going to happen, and there was nothing I could do about it.

Otto used a table on wheels, which was designed to go over the bed for a patient to put their glass of water or grapes, or whatever else they might have in this setting, on. He placed the briefcase on top and clicked open the catches before folding open the lid. I stared in horror. The case was lined with foam, and, placed into carefully cut out shapes in the foam, were several of the vials of what I assumed were the drug they would be giving me. He reached in and pulled out a syringe which was kept sterile in a paper and plastic packet. The needle was separate, a plastic cap covering the tip. The sight of it filled me with dismay.

I struggled in the chair, but Stewart held me down. "No, please, don't do this."

Otto wouldn't look at me.

"I can get you money," I blurted, trying to think of anything that might make him change his mind. If he was all about the work, then money might motivate him. "I'll sign my house over to you. Whatever it takes."

Infuriatingly, Hollan laughed. "Do you think I'm just going to let you walk out of here, so you can gazump me? Otto works for me. We have a contract, and he's already been paid. It doesn't matter what you offer him, this is still going to happen. He knows better than to go against me."

I thought I saw the slightest flicker of annoyance across Otto's face, but still he didn't say anything.

"Please," I begged Otto again, ignoring Hollan. "I'll give you anything you want. Anything. Just name it."

I knew begging was futile. Otto wouldn't be able to turn around and agree with me. There were three other men in this room, all of whom were armed. Even if Otto did decide to take my side, which I doubted he would, the two of us wouldn't be much use against the three of them and their guns.

I remembered the scissors still pressed against my ribcage. My body heat had warmed the metal. I'd need to use them soon, or it would be too late.

"I don't know," Stewart said from behind me, his fingers pressing into my shoulders, "she said *anything*. I think I'd be tempted to take her up on that. Have you gotten a decent look at that tight little body? Not sure I could resist the offer of making that bitch my own." I could hear the disgusting leer in his voice, and the fact that his hands were on me made my skin crawl.

I didn't know if Stewart was his first or last name. A part of me didn't care, but the other part thought that it might be important information for when I needed to track him down and kill him.

"This isn't a joke, Stewart," Hollan snapped. "Behave yourself."

Stewart had gotten himself all worked up at the idea of getting his hands on me, but now his ego deflated. "Sorry."

"How are you getting on there, Otto?" Hollan asked the Swede.

"Getting there," he replied, without looking around. He took the syringe out of the packet, then attached the needle to the end of the syringe, before breaking off the plastic cap. "I need someone to hold down her arm."

Bryson grabbed my left hand, pinning it, palm facing up, to the arm of the chair. The fingers of my right hand tingled, the metal of the scissors seeming to get hotter against my skin, telling me it was almost time.

Go for the eye or throat, I reminded myself. This might be my only chance at changing the course of things, and even though the thought made my stomach churn and acid burn up the lining of my throat, I had to be tough. Getting this wrong might mean the deaths of all those boys.

Stewart might be the one holding me down, but Otto was the one I needed to take down. He was the one about to inject me. Yes, the others might be able to muddle their way through without him, but I guessed by the fact they'd had to bring him in to do the job that it wasn't a simple as sticking a needle into a vein. There probably had to be correct dosages given at the right intervals to keep it working, and that took a specialist. In a way, I wished Otto hadn't given me the bottle of water earlier. This would have been a lot easier to do if he hadn't shown me that small amount of kindness.

He approached with the syringe and vial in one hand, a rubber tourniquet in the other. He wrapped the rubber around my upper arm and pulled it tight, pinching my skin. I could try to run again, but it would only buy me a matter of minutes, and they'd just grab me and haul me back here again. I needed to do something bigger, more permanent.

"Please, Otto. It's not too late to change your mind. Don't help him kill children. Please."

Otto didn't meet my eye, his pale blue gaze darting away from mine whenever it came near. I was giving him his last chance, too, only he didn't realize it, and I couldn't say anything out loud or I would be warning them all.

I watched every move he made, biding my time, waiting for the right moment.

He was focused, concentrating on finding a vein and piercing my skin with the needle. Every muscle in my body tensed, a wound coil ready to spring. My heart thrummed in my chest, my pulse racing. I had my shoulders pressed down against the back of the chair by Stewart, and Bryson held my left arm, but my right hand was free. I moved it slowly to my chest, as though clutching my breast in despair, and then I slipped my fingers into the V-neck of my shirt, reaching for the handles of the scissors.

I couldn't let myself think about it, how it would feel to have an eyeball burst beneath the sharp silver blades, the pop of fluid and membrane. I couldn't let myself think about what I had to do, or I was sure I'd back out.

Otto leaned in, his gaze focused on my skin, the needle point glinting in the sterile, bright light ...

With a shriek of rage, I snatched the scissors out of my bra and lunged forward. I'd caught Stewart by surprise once again, and he lost his grip on me. I stabbed at Otto's face, aiming for his eye, but he saw me coming, and reared back. My blades landed an inch off their mark, stabbing into his cheek instead. My fingers tightened around the handles, my screams of rage and horror filling my ears. I yanked downward, opening a flap in his skin, and then I was off the chair-bed, tumbling to the floor. Otto had dropped the syringe and vial, and it rolled close. Seeing an opportunity, even as the floor became smeared in red, blood pouring from Otto's ruined face, I lifted my foot and smashed it down onto the vial, shattering the glass into a thousand pieces.

All around me was carnage. The other men had pulled their weapons, but I didn't even care. I set my sights on the briefcase containing the other vials and threw myself at it. Bryson took after me, but slipped in Otto's blood, his feet flying up almost comically before he landed on his backside. My fingers caught the edge of the briefcase and it flipped up, turning through the air, before hitting the floor. The strike against the floor caused the vials to pop from their sponge casings, scattering everywhere. My gaze darted after them. I needed to destroy them. If there were no drugs, they'd have nothing to inject me with. How many had there been? My memory tried to process what I'd seen. Four in total? Three left in the case, that were now on the floor.

Otto was too preoccupied by the slash down his face to give a damn about me or the drugs. Hollan had pulled his weapon, but I didn't care about that. I was at the point of almost wanting him to shoot me just so this whole horror show would be over. I'd also noticed that Hollan, despite having killed my father, no longer appeared to want to get his hands dirty. I slammed my foot down on the second vial, and it went the same way as the first, and then scrambled for another that had rolled to a stop beneath the wheels of the table.

Stewart grabbed me, trying to haul me up. I fought against him, but he was a secondary concern. I needed to find that vial and destroy it. It was the last one, wasn't it? Had I missed one?

I spotted the final vial beneath the chair and I lunged.

My skin was slippery with Otto's blood. Stewart lost his grip on me, and I fell forward, landing on the vial that had almost gotten away. I managed to get my hand on it, when a weight from above crushed me. I'd been in the process of trying to pick the vial up from beneath me, but the sudden weight bent all my fingers into an unnatural position. I heard a sudden *pop* that went right down to the roots of my teeth, and agony lanced up through my hand and arm.

That wasn't good.

Chapter Nine

The pain shooting up through my hand and arm was excruciating. My mind flashed with bright white light, and I forgot everything else going on around me, existing only in that singular moment of agony. Then my body began to process all of the endorphins shooting through my veins to allow me to cope, and I slowly came back to reality.

Beneath my injured hand, the small glass vial pressed into my flesh. From the shape, I could tell it was still intact. Even though I was in agony, I couldn't let them save the vial. If they did, they would use it to inject me and this would have all been for nothing.

Stewart's weight on top of me shifted. The moment he got up and hauled me back to my feet, my chance would be gone. Yes, I could try to stamp on it, as I'd done with the other one, but if someone saw the intact vial first, they could easily snatch it out from under me.

"Get her up!" Hollan roared.

I couldn't think about it any longer. Despite knowing it was going to be agony, I pushed my injured hand down as hard as I could. A fresh burst of white hot pain shot through my hand, and I let out a scream, but I didn't stop, continuing to push down. The small glass tube fractured beneath my palm, glass sticking into my skin, though I barely noticed. My skin was wet with the contents of the vial, and I hoped none of the drug would get into my system through the cuts.

Stewart's hands around my upper arms dragged me back to my feet. I made the mistake of looking down at my hand and the world spun around me again. My little finger and ring finger were both bent at an unnatural angle—down and away from the other fingers.

Heat rushed through me and my mind pulled away from my surroundings. Though faint, I didn't want to pass out. The thought of being unconscious with these sons of bitches standing around me filled me with fear. I couldn't allow myself to be so vulnerable. I took a deep breath and looked away, not wanting to think too hard about what the unnatural bend to my fingers meant. Were they broken, or dislocated? I had no idea. I'd never broken anything in my life and didn't have any basis for comparison. Either way, it hurt like hell, and looked horrific.

The thought of something looking horrific made me think of Otto. I glanced over to where he stood, a sheet of red down the front of his shirt. He'd found a medical pad of some kind and had it folded and pressed to the wound I'd given him. Already the blood had soaked through the pad, and a streak of it had turned his white-blond hair pink. He was looking at me as though I'd morphed into something strange—something he suddenly didn't recognize. A surge of guilt rose up inside me, though I shouldn't feel guilty. He'd been working for Hollan and would have injected me with that stuff. He'd forced my hand.

"Get her back in the chair," Hollan commanded. "I need that code."

"She broke the vials," Otto said, though his voice was strange as he tried to speak without moving his face too much. He nodded toward the floor. "All of them. I do not have anything to give her."

Hollan turned his attention to me. "I guess you think that was smart, huh, Darcy? But you just removed the kind way of doing this. An injection would have been easy. You might have even enjoyed it. But instead, you have to make things difficult."

"Good," I spat. "I'll never make this easy for you."

His face turned puce with fury. With his stocky build, and hair cut so short it was almost shorn—like an Army buzz cut—he suddenly reminded me of an English Bulldog, and I had to hold back a snort of laughter. I was in no position to find anything funny, yet I couldn't help myself. The endorphins racing through my body were doing crazy things to my mind.

Hollan glanced down to my hand. "I think we need to give you a matching set of fingers on the other hand, just to remind you who's in control around here." He jerked his head at the two men. "Get her back in the chair."

To my surprise, neither of the men moved, and I stayed in the exact same position.

"Boss, I think Otto needs to be taken care of first." It was the first thing I'd heard Bryson say recently.

Hollan glanced over at the Swede. Otto's skin had faded beneath his tan, and the blood didn't look as though it was stopping any time soon. I recognized the indecisiveness of Hollan's face, as he tried to decide if torturing me was more important than having someone die of blood loss on his property.

"Dammit. Get her back to her room."

I had to stop myself from mouthing 'sorry' at Otto as Stewart and the other guy tightened their grip on me. I was starting to get used to the feel of their fingers around my arms, fingers digging into bruises over bruises. I didn't fight them this time. I was only glad they hadn't tried to grab my injured hand, which I cupped to my body, between my breasts. As well as Otto's face, I thought my fingers were also in need of medical attention, but I didn't think there was a chance of that happening any time soon. I'd have to try to figure it out by myself, though I had no idea what I was going to do. My mind pulled away from the edges every time my gaze strayed toward the way my fingers jutted out at a hideous angle from the rest of my hand.

Otto's blood covered my skin, but I doubted I was going to be allowed to clean myself off. I hadn't even been allowed to use a bathroom, and I figured that bucket was going to have to come into use sometime very soon.

Where the hell were the guys? I didn't want to think the tracker wasn't working, and they weren't coming. If I allowed my thoughts to take that route, I'd sink into despair. Now Hollan had the option of drugging me taken away, he was bound to go down the torture route. I figured we were in the middle of nowhere, and whatever concoction Otto had in the vials in the briefcase wouldn't be purchased in the local drugstore—not that I thought this place even had a local drug store. If I allowed myself to think they weren't coming, I knew I'd struggle to find the strength I needed to hold up against whatever Hollan did to me.

I wanted to be brave, wanted to be strong.

But everyone had their limits.

Stewart and Bryson dragged me back to the cell. The toes of my sneakers dragged on the ground as they moved with strides too long and fast to allow me to get my footing. We reached the cell, the door still standing open from where I'd been taken out of there. The two men hauled me back in, then threw me to the ground. Instinctively, I curled my body around my bad hand, trying to protect it as much as I could. I hit the floor on my side, jarring my shoulder and hip. Even though I hadn't hit my hand directly, a wave of sickening fresh pain permeated me at the movement, and my eyes flooded with tears. I blinked them away, not wanting Stewart to see them. There would be a time for crying and feeling sorry for myself, but it wouldn't be while these bastards were anywhere near me, taking pleasure from my tears.

I used my elbow and the side of the metal framed bed to drag myself up to a sitting position. I didn't quite trust my legs enough yet to stand, though I wished I could so I at least had the illusion that I was on an equal footing to these two thugs.

I thought the two men were going to leave me to it—prayed that's what they'd do—but Stewart paused and leaned in over me, his finger stabbed in my face. "Don't think you got one over on us, bitch. You're still our captive. We can do whatever the hell we want to you." His gaze flicked up and down the length of my body, and the tip of his tongue flicked out to lick at his skinny lips. I felt my whole body shrink inward, but I tried not to let my fear show.

"Fuck you."

"Listen to me, girly. We'll do whatever we want, and then we'll kill your pretty little ass."

I made myself sit up straighter, though it was hard to do with my poor hand tucked in against my body. "If that's going to happen anyway, you'd better go back and tell your boss that there is no way he's ever getting the code out of me. You've always got to give the person you want something from at least an inkling of hope that they'll get something in return—even if it's only a quick death. You just took everything off the table, and that means I don't have to tell Hollan shit."

I was probably doing completely the wrong thing by making the guy who already appeared to hate me even angrier, but I couldn't keep my mouth shut. I wanted to give him something to think about, to make him realize he hadn't won. I thought Stewart was one of those men who intrinsically hated women. He only ever wanted to fuck us, and then probably hated himself for doing it. If I was a betting girl, I'd have put a couple of grand down on him having an unhealthy relationship with his mother. Luckily, I managed to keep that little thought to myself. It probably would have earned me a busted nose if I hadn't.

"Oh, you'll talk," he snarled. "We've broken grown men in the past. Don't think for one minute you won't tell us everything we want to know."

I clamped my lips shut. There was no point arguing with the son of a bitch. I'd make sure he paid for every threat he threw at me as soon as the guys arrived.

Together with Hollan, Stewart was definitely on my 'men I planned to kill' list.

To my relief, he gave up threatening me and backed out of the room. He slammed the door, the lock cracking into place, and I was able to breathe again. Just.

My attention went to my hand, and the sight sent fresh fear through me. I took little gasps of air, my eyes pricking with the tears I'd held back for so long. I wished I was one of those women who watched endless medical dramas, so maybe I would have had some idea about what had happened to my hand.

Though I didn't want to, I forced myself to look more closely. I couldn't leave it like that. If it was broken, the fingers needed to be strapped so they didn't heal in that position—assuming I lived long enough for them to heal, that was.

I swiped at my tears with my other hand, and then grimaced as the tears mixed with Otto's blood, which had been slowly drying on my skin. Knowing I was procrastinating from what really needed to be dealt with, I used my good hand to reach beneath the thin mattress and locate the half-drunk bottle of water. Though I hated to waste the only water I had—and knowing it was highly unlikely Otto would ever bring me another bottle—I still had to get Otto's blood off my skin. The sight of it reminded me too much of the night my father had died, how his blood had covered every inch of my arms and hands.

As though the sight sent me tumbling down a rabbit hole of memories, my thoughts went to the days and weeks after my father had been killed. It had been as though my brain had been unable to process what had happened, and that I'd had a bad dream and expected to wake up at any moment. Or that I'd be able to rewind time and make it as though it had never happened. I'd kept expecting to see him in places where he'd normally be—in the kitchen first thing in the morning, making coffee, or walking through the door at the end of the day. Aunt Sarah had moved in straight after he'd been killed, and I'd found that I'd hear her moving around the house, and each time I expected it to be him, but of course it never was. My brain had always taken a moment to catch up with reality, the lift of thinking I'd see him, followed by the instant dip of disappointment, and then a punch of grief, causing my chest to physically ache. Had I hated her a little back then for never being him? For always getting my hopes up, only to be the one to, however unintentionally, dash them again?

I'd questioned every step I'd taken that day, and even things I'd done in the days and weeks and months before he'd been killed, wondering if something I had done or could have done might have had a domino effect. If I hadn't been late home a few nights earlier, we wouldn't have been fighting about him not allowing me to go to a party that night, and he might have not been in that room at that time, or his attention might not have been on me, so he'd have heard the killer coming. Even down to ridiculous things, like wishing we hadn't switched the furniture around the previous year, as he'd been standing where the couch used to be. If he'd been standing somewhere slightly different maybe the bullet wouldn't have killed him.

I was trying to make sense of it, hoping there was a way of changing the past, all the while filled with the futility of knowing nothing could ever change. He was gone. There was no bringing him back.

I sniffed back fresh tears. I thought after this many years, I could still think of what had happened without wanting to cry, but I guessed considering the situation, I was allowed a few tears.

Taking a couple more shuddery breaths, I pulled myself together. As much as I wanted to wallow in self-pity, I knew it wouldn't get me anywhere. The sharp agony of my hand had dulled to a steady throb, but it still hurt like hell, and every time I glanced at my fingers, a wash of nausea flashed hot and cold through my body.

I moved my attention back to the bottle of water. Clamping the bottle between my knees, I used my left hand to unscrew the top. I picked up the bottle with my uninjured hand and splashed a little on the cuts caused by the broken vial. Washing the blood off my left hand proved to be trickier, but I managed to pinch the neck between the thumb and forefinger of my right hand to lift the bottle, careful not to bump my injured fingers, and then tipped a little water on my bloodied hand and arm.

The only material I had in the cell, other than my own clothes, was the mattress behind me, so I twisted around and used the side of it to wipe the worst of the blood off.

The job was far from perfect, and I'd have given anything for a bar of soap and running water, but it would have to do. With my skin relatively clean, I turned my attention to my fingers. If they were broken, they'd be bent at the break in the bone, I assumed. I forced myself to look. As far as I could tell, the bend was at the first knuckle of both fingers. Did that mean they were dislocated rather than broken? If so, would I be able to pop them back into place?

The thought made me sick and dizzy, but I wouldn't be able to use the hand unless I did something about it. If Isaac and the others ever showed up, I was going to need to run, and quite possibly fight, and I wasn't going to be able to do anything while I worried about protecting my hand.

If I was wrong, however, and the fingers were broken rather than dislocated, this was going to hurt like hell.

Chapter Ten

I'd never experienced real pain before—not physical pain, anyway. Emotional pain, I'd had by the bucket load, but this was different. This was going to hurt like hell, and I wasn't ashamed to admit the thought of the pain terrified me. I wished there was another option, but there wasn't. At some point, I was going to need to run or fight, and I wouldn't be able to do either with my fingers sticking out like that. They almost looked as though they didn't belong to me, as though I was looking at puppet fingers, or even a Halloween prop. They'd started to swell and had taken on a strange pale hue, which did nothing to help the way my brain wanted to disconnect from them.

But they were mine, and I needed to do something about it, even if the idea made me want to pass out, and I wanted to wail and beat the floor with my good hand, and cry about how unfair all of this was. I just needed to grit my teeth and get on with it. The longer I waited, the worse it would be.

I remembered what I'd done while I'd been locked in the trunk of Hollan's car, how I'd used my thoughts of the guys to ease the trauma, and I willed my mind to take me there again. My happy place. With all of them.

I closed my eyes and pictured them around me ...

Alex came to me first, tall and blond, his expression serious as he looked down at my injured hand. "It's definitely dislocated, Darc," he told me. "But that's good. It means you can fix it, and the pain will get one hundred times better. You just have to do exactly what I say."

I nodded. I would do that. I would do exactly as he said.

Kingsley was the next to appear. "And remember to breathe," he told me in his deep, chocolate smooth voice. "You don't want to pass out, and you'll regain more control if you take a deep breath in right before you have to put the fingers back into place, and exhale as you're doing it. Okay?"

"Okay," I whispered.

Isaac appeared by the door, crouching to peer through the crack in the hatch, checking out the corridor beyond. "You have to get on with it, love. They might be back at any moment, and then you'll have lost your chance."

I looked back down at my hand and gave a whine of pain and fear. I didn't want to do this, but I knew I had to.

A hand pressed on my shoulder, giving me a reassuring squeeze, and I looked up into Lorcan's hazel eyes. "You can do this, princess, I know you can."

I nodded. "Thanks, Lorcan."

"We're all here for you. You know that."

Clay appeared in front of me, nodding as he pushed a hand through his hair. "Yeah, we're here for you. Now stop being such a drama queen and get on with it."

I gave a small laugh. Tough love. I knew what he was doing, but I also caught the little glimpse of sadness in his blue eyes.

"Okay, okay, I'm doing it."

Alex spoke again. "You're going to need to press against the bone where it's dislocated, to make sure it's not caught against the side of the joint, and then pull outward before putting it back in place."

"And remember to breathe," said Kingsley. "Take hold of the finger, take a deep breath in, and sharp exhale while you move it."

I nodded, and Lorcan squeezed my shoulder again. I wished I could ask one of them to do it for me, but they were all in my imagination, and such a thing was impossible.

Both hands trembled as I took hold of my bent little finger with the opposite hand. I needed to follow Alex's direction and pull outward to open up the joint again, and push it back into place.

I just needed to do it. If I kept thinking too hard, I'd end up chickening out.

Gritting my jaw, I tightened my hold on my little finger. I took a deep breath in, and as I exhaled, I pulled.

Pain shot up through my arm, and I clamped my scream between my teeth. I released my finger and felt the pop as it went back into the joint. I panted hard, perspiration popping on my brow and upper lip. But the pain emanating from my pinky finger began to fade, and I dared to look down. It was back in position, and already color started to flood back into the digit.

"Well done," said Alex. "You're almost finished. Just the next one to go, and you'll be done."

Isaac checked the corridor again. "Get on with it, love."

I looked back down at my hand. The pinky finger was a hundred times better. My ring finger, however, still didn't look great. I felt sick from the pain, and knowing I was going to have to put myself through it again. But I had to do it.

I took another couple of deep breaths and took hold of my ring finger. I was careful of my newly aligned pinky finger as well, not wanting to push it out of joint again. A strange squealing noise pealed from my throat as I squeezed my eyes shut and pulled. The pain was blinding, and my eyes rolled and the world pulled away at the edges. But I couldn't pass out with this only half done, and I kept going, clamping my teeth together and yanking with a hard tug. The finger popped back into place and I curled over, cupping my hurt hand with the other one, breathing hard and waiting for the pain to fade.

Finally, it did, and I looked up to discover the guys had all gone. I knew they hadn't been real, but I still missed their presence. It was stupid—my mind playing tricks on me—but having them here, reassuring me, had almost felt real. Missing them hit me like a blow to the chest, and I took a shaky breath, trying to position myself back in reality. The few imaginary moments with the guys had done what it needed to, and given me the strength I'd required to help my hand, but I needed to face reality now.

I risked looking down at the hand again. It looked almost normal, though the joints were swollen, but I could live with that. I didn't want to risk hurting it again. I should bind the injured fingers to the good ones, now that they were back in the right position, but I didn't have anything to bind them with. The only material in the room were the clothes I wore.

I glanced down at my jeans and t-shirt. The jeans were too thick for me to rip, so that only left the top. I lifted the bottom of my t-shirt, and, using my teeth, tore a strip from the bottom. It meant my stomach was exposed, but I preferred that to having to see my digits in that position again.

Using the strip of t-shirt, I wrapped the two fingers against my middle one, so all three were strapped together. It was a fiddly process, and I had to use my teeth again, together with my other hand, to tie a knot and keep the makeshift bandage secure. Having all the fingers in the right position had made me feel better, and now they were also hidden from view and feeling snug and secure beneath the bandage, I was finally able to breathe again.

My racing heart began to slow, and my eyes slipped shut. I was exhausted and shaky, and I needed to rest. The metal bed frame with the thin, dirty mattress was right beside me, but I still didn't want to climb onto it. Giving in to sleep somehow also felt as though I was giving up. Sleeping meant being exposed and vulnerable, and though my eyes were sore, my lids heavy with exhaustion, I continued to fight against it. Even so, my thoughts drifted, and I barely noticed the cold, concrete floor beneath me. The faces of the men I waited for flitting in and out of my mind—Clay ... Lorcan ... Kingsley ... Alex ... Isaac ... Thinking of them was like wrapping myself in a warm, weighted blanket—

The click of the lock pulled me from my reverie, and I gave a groan. I only wanted to be left alone and escape into my fantasy world. I'd slumped while lost in thought, but I instantly straightened at the sound of the door, my pulse quickening. Was Hollan back again? What did he plan on doing with me now? I was sure he'd punish me for what I'd done to Otto and for breaking the vials. I'd ruined his plans, and Hollan wasn't the type of man to allow a thing like that to go lightly.

The door opened a crack, as though the person behind didn't want to be seen, and then a body slipped into the space. The light in the corridor outside was brighter than inside my cell, so at first it was hard to make out who my visitor was, but then my heart sank.

Stewart.

The concrete floor was cold beneath me and had leached through to my bones, so every ache and pain magnified ten times over. Damp permeated the air. Though my body hurt, I scrambled to my feet, not wanting to be found in a position of vulnerability while this man was occupying the same space as I was. There were plenty of dangerous men around, but some men were more dangerous than others. It was the way they looked at women, as though they believed the females of the species were automatically below them in the pecking order. That kind of arrogance was never good for the woman.

"Hello, Darcy,"

He moved farther into the room and pulled the door shut behind him. My gaze locked on that door. My only route to freedom closed off.

I cupped my bad hand against my body. "What do you want, Stewart?"

"I thought we might have a little chat."

"I don't have anything to say to you. Does Hollan know you're in here?"

Stewart shrugged. "He doesn't need to know."

I took a step back, toward the rear of the room, and Stewart stepped forward, matching mine. My heart raced. "Hollan's not going to like it if you hurt me," I spluttered, feeling as though my words were empty. Truthfully, I wasn't sure if Hollan gave a shit or not. It wasn't as though the other man was taking care of me.

A salacious smile spread across his snake-like face. "Oh, no one said anything about hurting you, Darcy. I want to make you feel good. Don't you want a break from all of this? Just lie back and let me make you forget where you are for a while."

"Don't come any closer!" Panic heightened my tone.

He laughed. "Or what?"

"I'll scream."

"You think people are going to help you? After what you just did? Have you forgotten where you are? You were screaming and crying earlier, and no one came to help you, did they? What makes you think anything has changed now?"

With sickening dread, I realized he was right.

My gaze darted around, desperate for something I could use as a weapon, but there was nothing. I only had myself—my teeth, feet, and hands, and even one of those wasn't working properly. I'd fight with every part of me before I let this man touch me.

He stepped forward again, and I moved back, but this time my back hit the wall behind. He was quite literally backing me into a corner.

I opened my mouth and yelled. "Help! Someone help me!" Then something in my head clicked and I remembered how you should never yell help when you really needed it. "Fire!" I screamed instead, the word grating my throat. "Fire!"

"Shut up, bitch," Stewart snarled, and then he lunged for me.

I was ready for him and sidestepped, but he managed to snag my t-shirt, yanking me back. My neck snapped with whiplash, but that was the least of my concerns. Stewart launched his entire bodyweight at me, throwing me to the floor, so I smacked my chin on the ground. I'd managed to protect my bad hand with the other one, but pain still shattered through me at the impact. I was hardly given time to process what was happening as he landed on top of me, crushing the air from my lungs before I even got the chance to move or fight back. His hand grabbed the back of my head, his fingers traversing my skull, and he mashed my face into the ground. I'd promised myself I'd fight, but in this position, with my face down, and his body pinning me, I felt as helpless as a hooked fish left flapping on a pier. The noise that came out of my throat was a frightened whine. I tried to struggle, but I was terrifyingly powerless.

He leaned over me, and his breath was hot against the back of my ear, the tepid stench of stale cigarette smoke wafting over me, making me want to gag. "Oh, yeah, baby," he rasped, his mouth so close to my ear, as his lips grazed my lobe. "Keep struggling like that. It only turns me on more."

The weight alleviated a fraction, but was replaced by tugging at my jeans. He was trying to pull them down, and then he'd rape me from behind, with my face mashed against the cold, damp floor, and I'd never be the same person again.

I wriggled and bucked the best I could. Horror that this might actually happen made me blind with panic. I didn't think I could string a coherent thought together. I suddenly understood how women often said they simply froze when they were threatened with being raped. That they felt guilty they hadn't fought back, but yet hadn't been able to when it happened.

All I could manage was a panicked whine, and the sound of it frightened me as much as anything else. The voice didn't even sound as though it belonged to me. "No, please. Stop, no, no ..."

"That's it, bitch," Stewart said, and I could hear amusement in his voice. "Keep begging like that. I love to hear you beg."

The door opened, bright light flooding in a shaft across the concrete floor. My breath caught, wondering who had walked in. Would it be someone to help me, or someone who'd make things even worse, if that was possible?

"What the fuck?"

I recognized the accent. Otto. I almost cried with relief. From my position where I'd been thrown, I was able to lift my head enough to see the other man. I was looking at him from the feet up, so his legs appeared impossibly long, his shoulders and head miles away.

Otto shot me a look, and I tried not to stare at the tape across his face, holding down a bandage that no doubt covered whatever stitches they'd been able to do. He wasn't at a hospital, then? The cut I'd given him would leave him with one hell of a fearsome scar if it went without the attention of a plastic surgeon.

"Get lost," Stewart snapped. "This is none of your concern."

Otto took another step into the cell. "It looks like it should be my concern."

"Please," I begged, though my voice came out muffled as I had to speak against the floor. "He's trying to rape me." I knew I was begging to the same man whose face I'd slashed open only a couple of hours earlier, but he was my only chance. I'd never gotten the same vibe from Otto as I had from Stewart, and, if it wasn't for the whole 'trying to drug me' thing, I would have assumed him to be an ally.

Stewart shoved his hand down harder on the back of my head, mashing my face into the concrete. It wasn't me he addressed next, however. "Don't pretend like this isn't something you've thought about yourself, dude. What harm's it gonna do? Not like she's gonna walk out of this place, anyway."

Otto's ice blue eyes narrowed. They looked almost supernatural in the dim light. "I do not rape women."

"You fucking hypocrite. But you inject them with some concoction of drugs, and then walk away to let men like Hollan do whatever they want."

"That is not the same thing. Let Darcy get up."

"Make me."

I'd stopped squirming, instead frozen beneath Stewart's hold, every muscle tensed as I waited to hear my fate. I wanted more than anything to use the moment to try to elbow the son of a bitch in the face, but I didn't want to give Otto any reason to step in and take Stewart's side.

"I will not say it again," the Swede said. "Let her go. Hollan will not like it if he finds out you threatened to kill her when it was done."

"I never said that," he blustered, but his hold on me had weakened. "Hollan will let me do anything I want to her once we get the information out of her."

"And what if raping her leaves her so traumatized she cannot speak, or she forgets the numbers? How do you think your boss is going to react then?"

A growl came from above, but then the hand lifted off the back of my head, and I was able to move. Stewart got to his feet, and I scrambled away from him, secreting myself into a corner. My arms wrapped around my legs, my knees drawn up to my chest in protection.

Stewart looked at me and jabbed a finger in my direction. "As soon as Hollan gets what he wants, I'll have your ass. Got it?"

I scowled at him, but didn't answer. That certainly was never going to motivate me into giving Hollan what he wanted.

Stewart left the room, pushing past Otto to get out of the door. The Swede with the pale blue eyes and almost white hair stood his ground, ignoring the other man's aggression. Otto waited until he was gone and stepped into the room. He must have seen me cower back, as he lifted his hand in surrender. "It is okay. I will not hurt you. I want only to check that you are all right."

"Clearly, I'm not," I muttered, leaning away from him and pulling my knees tighter against my chest.

A troubled expression crossed his face, his lips pressed together, his pale eyebrows drawn down. My gaze fixed on the white bandage on the side of his face. I couldn't believe he'd helped me, even after I'd hurt him so badly. I wouldn't have blamed him if he'd either walked away and pretended he hadn't come in when he had, or else joined in with Stewart by way of revenge. It said a lot about a man's integrity when he was willing to protect a woman who had hurt him.

Otto looked as though he was thinking something, but then he shook his head and turned away.

"Otto, wait!" I cried, reaching out for him with my good hand. I didn't know how much more I expected from him, perhaps hoping he might sneak me out of this place, but he didn't even pause at my cry. Instead, he stepped through the door and pulled it shut behind him. He snapped the lock back into place, leaving me alone once more.

Despite my earlier insistence to myself that I would never sleep on the horrible bed, I found myself crawling up onto it and slumping down onto my side, my hand, which was throbbing, held out in front of me. My eyes were sore and heavy from crying, my brain foggy. Though the mattress was thin, and I could feel the metal springs of the fold out bed beneath, my body relaxed. The mattress seemed to vanish, with me sinking deeper and deeper into it, my mind too exhausted to even think, and before I had even registered I was falling, I was already asleep.

Chapter Eleven

My dreams took me away from my damaged body and horrific surroundings.

"Hey, sugar."

His voice was soft, but I recognized it instantly. I spun to face him. "Clay!"

He was standing in front of me, in his baggy jeans and t-shirt. He pushed his hand through his jaw-length blond hair and looked up at me from under it.

"I thought you were never going to come."

He gave me a slow smile. "Of course we were. We'd never leave you, baby-doll."

I looked around. "Where are the others?"

"We're right here, princess." My heart soared. Lorcan.

I turned again to find him standing there, all leather jacketed, dark hair, and smoldering.

"Lorcan, are you okay? How is your shoulder?"

He shrugged. "It's fine. I told you it would be. Takes a little more than a bullet to keep me down."

A third voice came from over my shoulder. "Didn't you trust that I'd make him better?" I spun around again to find Alex grinning at me. I knew he was only teasing.

"Of course I did. I trusted you, Alex. I can't tell you how happy I am you're here." His tall, blond haired, blue eyed good looks shimmered before me as tears trembled in my eyes.

I felt like there was something I wanted Alex to look at for me, but I couldn't think what it was. Had I dreamed it?

Someone else stepped out from the shadows. Kingsley. "You getting yourself in trouble again, Darcy?"

I hitched a little sob of happiness. "Yeah, I think maybe I was. But I'm okay now."

He put his arms out to me, and before I registered either of us moving, I was in them, protected through the sheer size of him, my face pressed against his solid chest.

I realized someone was still missing, and I forced myself to lift my head from Kingsley's chest. "Where's Isaac?"

"I'm right here, love."

I twisted in Kingsley's arms to face him, my heart lifting. If Isaac was here, it meant we'd be okay. We were all meant to be together—we could take on anything if we were together—and now we were, and my heart felt whole again.

Kingsley released me, allowing me to go to Isaac. A few fast paces brought me in front of him. He caught my face in both hands and kissed me in a way he never had before, deep and intense, as though I was the love of his life who he hadn't seen for months on end. I kissed him in return, my fingers lacing around the back of his neck, into the soft, silky strands of his hair. I didn't care that the others were all watching; why would I? I'd kiss any of them in exactly the same way.

A body pressed up behind me, sandwiching me between Isaac. The gentle brush of fingertips scooped my hair away from the back of my neck. Warm lips placed soft kisses to my nape, and I shivered in the best way possible. Who did the kisses belong to? Lorcan? Alex? Kingsley? Clay?

I stopped kissing Isaac long enough to glance over my shoulder. Blue eyes, tall, lanky frame.

Alex.

He gave me a smile that was almost apologetic, and I reached behind me to pull him closer, dragging his hips against the small of my back, to show him it was okay.

But someone else caught my hand, and my fingers were pressed to soft, full lips. I glanced over to see Kingsley with his mouth to my hand, and, as I watched, he drew my middle finger into his mouth, grating at it gently with his teeth, swirling his hot wet tongue around the tip. The sight and sensations sent a pulse of desire through me, heat pooling between my thighs. I still had Isaac pressing against me from the front, Alex behind. Alex's kisses drifted across my neck, but then I realized someone else had joined him—Lorcan. Alex was kissing one side of my neck, Lorcan the other.

Isaac tipped my chin up to him, and kissed me again.

Then Clay was there, too, on the opposite side from Kingsley, kissing the back of my hand and up my arm.

A little moan of pleasure escaped my lips. This was how I'd always fantasized about this happening, all five guys on me at once, their hands caressing me, their mouths kissing, tasting, licking. I could feel the hardness of Isaac's erection pressing into my stomach as his tongue pushed into my mouth, and Lorcan's cock was rigid against my left hip, Alex, being taller, ground himself against the dip of my waist. I wanted to have them all, in my hands, my mouth, inside me. Everywhere. Using me, taking me, making me theirs.

Only, this wasn't real, was it? This wasn't really happening.

The thought sent something like a jolt of electricity through me. Why did I think that? Of course it was real.

And yet something had resonated within me, something deep in my brain picking up on that thought and clinging to it like a drowning man at a life raft.

"It's okay, Darc," Alex said between kisses. "We're here. We came for you."

But the sense of unease didn't fade, and I found myself pulling away, trying to shrug him off, but I couldn't. Each of the men pressed in on every side, trapping me between them. What was happening? Something was very wrong. My pulse began to race, and, instead of feeling sexy and protected, I only felt claustrophobic and trapped. Yes, trapped. That was what I was.

"No, please, you have to let me go. Something's wrong."

I pushed against Isaac, but he didn't budge. "Stop it, love. We're here, we have you now."

I shook my head, tears pouring down my cheeks. "No, this is all wrong. All of it. You haven't come for me. You left me. You never came!"

I BURST FROM SLEEP, gasping for breath, and already sitting upright on the thin, dirty mattress. The first thing I became aware of was the throbbing in my hand. The second was that my face was wet with tears.

I'd been crying in my sleep.

My chest ached at the realization none of the guys was here. Had they given up on me completely? Or did they simply not know where I was?

I lifted my good hand and touched the tracker still behind my ear. How many hours had passed since I'd handed myself over to Hollan? Twelve hours? Less? I had no way of knowing the time, but either way, Isaac and the others should have reached me by now.

Unless something bad had happened to them? A twinge of worry and guilt went through me. I hadn't considered that before. What if Hollan had already predicted Isaac and the rest of the guys would come after me, and had put plans in place to prevent that from happening? He might have others lying in wait on the road, ready to take out the entire van and everyone inside it. I'd been thinking about myself this entire time, but what if my hopes for rescue were pointless because the guys were already dead?

Ice water rushed through my veins at the thought. My dream clung to me, and I was filled with a sudden desperation to lie back down on the dirty mattress and vanish into my dream world again, to hang onto the men—or at least my illusion of them. The thought of them being dead made me want to curl up into a ball and give up. What would be the point in carrying on fighting if they were never going to come?

The pull of despair tried to drag me under, but I fought against it. My mind was doing cruel things to me again, and I needed to think more rationally.

If the guys were dead, I was sure Hollan would have crowed about it. Hell, he'd probably have brought the bodies here for me to see, just to impound my misery. I don't know what I ever did to him to make him hate me—apart from having a father who betrayed him, of course—but his hatred of me felt personal.

Even if I was in this alone, I still had to make sure Hollan never got the code from me. Perhaps it would be better if I did die. Then the code would die with me, and so would everyone's access to the locations of the other bases. Yes, Devlin said it was vitally important for them to be able to contact the other bases in case of an extreme emergency, but they'd lasted this long without doing so. Wasn't it better to let it go, and in doing so prevent people like Hollan trying to take them out? I knew Devlin would argue that it wasn't, but I wasn't so sure. The safety of those children was surely more important than the coordination of the job they were being raised for.

No, the guys were coming for me. I had to keep believing that. They'd been held up by something, but they'd do everything in their power to find me again. I needed to stick to my side of the plan.

I needed to find the flash drive. Or if I could get to the phone again, I'd be able to try to call Aunt Sarah's cell. Just because it had gone straight through to her voicemail the previous time didn't mean it wasn't working. The phone might have run out of charge, or she might be in a different location now. There were plenty of possibilities. Hearing her voice again would help to renew my strength and determination. I didn't want to die. I wanted to go on and live my life—a life far greater than I'd ever considered possible only a matter of a couple of weeks ago. Everything had changed now, and I wanted to be back with the guys again, and for us to figure out our futures from there—assuming we had one together.

I swung my legs off the side of the bed and got to my feet. My legs felt shaky, and my knuckles were bruised and swollen to twice their size, but I was otherwise okay. Something else pressed at me, though, and I wrinkled my nose thinking about it. My bladder strained uncomfortably, and I knew I was going to have to empty it before I'd be able to concentrate on anything else. Even after all of the kidnapping, and Stewart trying to rape me, and the number of times I'd been bound and beaten, somehow being forced to use a bucket felt like the ultimate humiliation.

I was pretty sure Hollan didn't have any cameras in here, so that was something, at least. Even so, just in case, I picked up the bucket and took it to the darkest corner. I shouldn't care about someone wanting to watch me piss in a bucket—if that was their thing, they had more issues than I did to worry about—but I wanted that tiny bit of privacy.

I used my left hand to pop the button on my jeans, then pushed them, together with my panties, down to my ankles. This was going to be awkward, and the last thing I wanted to do was piss on my jeans. I felt horribly exposed and wanted to get this over with as quickly as possible.

Using the wall beside me to support myself, I squatted over the bucket. At first, I didn't think my bladder was going to let go—I was suffering from stage fright, even though I didn't think anyone was watching—but then a hot rush of urine crashed into the metal bucket, and I was able to exhale a sigh of relief.

With no tissue, I was forced to shake off, and I quickly yanked my underwear and jeans back up. I didn't want to stay in this room, especially now I could smell my own piss, on top of everything else. Otto's blood, where I'd wiped it off my hands, still stained the mattress, and the thought of it caused a shudder to vibrate down my spine.

I had to do something. I couldn't stay in here.

Crossing the room, I went to the door. With my good hand, I banged on the door, and then pressed my mouth against the gap in the hatch. "Hey! Hollan! You out there? I want to make a deal."

My stomach churned at the prospect. This could all go horribly wrong. So far, my plans hadn't been working out too well for me, but I'd never been the type of person to sit back and do nothing. I didn't want to have to face Stewart and Bryson either, but I needed to make sure Hollan had the memory stick here. The guys would be coming, and I wanted to point them directly to it when they did.

"I can't do this anymore. Please. I just want out." I normally wasn't any good at crying on command, but my emotions were already frayed, and I was hungry and humiliated, and in pain.

"Hello? I know you're there. Can you hear me, Hollan? I'm done fighting. You can have the code."

I listened hard for footsteps. Where the hell was everyone? Had they left me here alone? I wasn't sure how I felt about that, if they had. Part jubilation that I no longer inhabited the same space as my father's murderer, but part fear that I was alone and locked in a cell. What if there was a fire, or someone else found this place and came in to hurt me?

No, I didn't think Hollan would leave me here unsupervised, would he? Maybe he figured I was locked up, so I couldn't get into any trouble.

Or perhaps they were simply all asleep. I had no clock or windows, so couldn't tell if it was morning or night. I suspected it was night, but I could have slept right through and not realized. I hadn't seen any bedrooms in this place, though. It wasn't like the base, where it was equipped for people to live—or at least not that I'd seen. So maybe they'd left to go back to their homes? As far as I knew, Hollan was single, unless he'd met and married someone in recent years, and didn't have anyone to go home to, but what about the others? I hated to think of Stewart having a family somewhere. That man didn't deserve any kind of happiness, and I doubted he'd treat a wife or children with any kindness.

But then I heard the hollow click of a door opening, followed by footsteps farther down the corridor. Someone was coming.

I renewed my efforts, lifting my voice higher, pressing my lips against the gap in the hatch. "Hollan? Hey, I'm ready to talk. Are you there?"

I waited for an answer, but there wasn't one. Instead, the footsteps grew closer, and I straightened and stepped back from the door, my breath caught in my lungs.

"What do you want, Darcy?" Hollan's tone was hard, no-nonsense. "We're busy trying to clean up your mess."

Did he mean Otto? Had I not been asleep for long, then? I'd always found it hard to distinguish whether I'd slept for one hour or six. It was the one time my synesthesia let me down.

"I want to cut a deal," I called through the door.

I could hear the suspicion in his voice. "What kind of a deal?"

"I'll give you the code, as long as I get to be the one who enters it."

His suspicion deepened. "And why would you want to do that?"

"I want to know what's on there. I want to know what my father gave his life to protect."

"They never told you?"

I knew exactly who he was talking about when he said 'they.' "No. Why would they? They just saw me as some girl who had something they wanted, exactly the same as you. Are you about to tell me what's on it?"

"No, I'm not."

"But what if I gave you the code?"

Silence met my ears, and I knew he was thinking about my offer.

"Come on," I tried to prod him. "It's not as though I have a whole lot I can get back in return, and I know you're not going to let me walk from this. A little information is the only thing I'm asking for in return, and it's not as though I'm going to get the opportunity to use it."

He paused, and I didn't think he was going to reply, but then he said, "Why the sudden change of heart?"

"I got hurt. Other people are getting hurt. Honestly, I'm exhausted, and I just want this to be over." I conjured my tears and took a hitching breath, sniffing. When I spoke again, my voice broke. "I still miss my dad. At least soon this will all be over, and we'll be together again." My words caused a swell of sadness to rise inside of me, and I barked out a genuine sob, before pressing my fingers to my lips to hold it in. For some reason, I didn't care about faking my misery to Hollan, but showing him genuine emotion made me feel like I was exposing myself. Exposing my weaknesses.

Only silence met my ears once again, and I stared at the door, wishing I could see Hollan's expression and gauge his reaction. Was he giving a snide smile and shaking his head, already figuring he was onto me? Or was he biting his lower lip and frowning at the door, falling for my misery and considering taking my offer? After all, they no longer had Otto's drug to make me tell the truth about the code, and I had no idea how long it would take for them to get more—might be weeks, for all I knew. They could go down the torture route—hell, Hollan would probably even enjoy that, and I was sure Stewart would—but that also took time and would most likely get messy. And there was always the risk that something goes wrong, and I might die from whatever they did to me rather than hand over what they wanted.

But then movement came, and, instead of a response, I heard footsteps fading away. I no longer got any sense of him standing outside the door. Dammit. Had I tried too hard? He hadn't bought my little act, and I was now stuck in the same position, completely useless, sitting in this damned cell and waiting for whatever he decided to do with me next.

From somewhere in the building came the bang of doors, followed by the low monotone of male voices.

I let out a growl and slammed my balled fist against the door, before lowering my forehead to join it. I'd hoped Hollan might have taken the easier route, but I'd obviously put up too much of a fight so far, and so he didn't trust a word I said. Not that I blamed him. I wouldn't trust me either. He was now obviously leaving me here to stew before he decided which parts of me he started cutting off first to get me to give up the code.

But on the other side of the door, something changed.

My stomach flipped, and I lifted my forehead back up. Both the footsteps and the voices seemed to be getting closer. Hollan was coming back.

My heart pattered in my chest, and I snatched a breath as I took a step back. From what I could hear, the men had reached the door and were now paused on the other side.

The lock was pushed back with a crack.

Chapter Twelve

The door opened to reveal Hollan. Stewart and Bryson lurked in the corridor close behind. The sight of Stewart turned my stomach, but I wasn't going to let them see they'd fazed me.

Remembering I was supposed to be brokenhearted and contemplating my own mortality, I swiped at the tears on my face with my hand and lowered my gaze to look at the floor. Inside, however, my heart thrummed in anticipation. If Hollan was going to take me to the memory stick, didn't it mean the stick was in this building? I'd have done what I'd planned when I'd first made the decision to hand myself over to Hollan in return for Aunt Sarah. I'd planned to find the location of the flash drive, and now that plan was about to come to fruition. I hadn't quite figured out what I'd do when I was faced with the memory stick, but I'd have to work that out. Right now, destroying it seemed like the best option, though I doubted I'd be given the opportunity, and I knew Isaac, Devlin, and the others would be hugely disappointed in me if they found out that was what I'd done.

Worry wound its way across my heart. Would it mean the end of my time with Isaac and the guys? If they discovered I'd deliberately damaged the memory stick, would they call it a day on their relationships with me? I'd have taken away the only chance they'd ever find the locations of bases like theirs. Surely that would be unforgivable?

I didn't know why I was worrying about it. I doubted Hollan would let me live long enough to continue whatever was going on between me and the guys. That seriously needed to be the least of my worries right now.

A thought occurred to me. My father had designed the code so if it were entered incorrectly, all the information would be wiped from the memory stick. All I needed to do was give Hollan the wrong number, and he'd wipe the memory stick himself. I wondered why he hadn't considered the possibility of me doing such a thing. Was it because he believed my loyalty to the guys was stronger than my will to bring this whole thing to an end? Or was it because he'd simply kill me if I did such a thing?

No, Hollan thought I wanted to know what was on the drive, too. If I wanted that, I needed to give him the correct code. Putting in the wrong one would wipe the information from me as well.

Hollan jerked his chin to tell me to step forward.

Stewart also took a step toward me, but Hollan put out his hand to stop him. "She's coming willingly this time, aren't you, Darcy?"

I kept my head down, my eyes training on the ground. I nodded. Honestly, it was enough to agree to it just to keep Stewart's damned hands off me.

"Good," Hollan said.

They all turned, walking down the corridor, with Hollan leading the way. I wondered what had happened to Otto. Had he left this place now? Gone to get some proper medical attention? I hoped he had. Yes, he'd tried to inject me, and was working for Hollan, but if he hadn't saved me from Stewart, I thought I'd most likely be a changed person right now. A woman didn't live through something like that—if they even survived—and not come out of it with something inside her fundamentally broken. A different kind of man would have conceded that I deserved everything coming to me after I'd cut up his face, but Otto hadn't. He still stepped in, and though I had no idea where he was now, I was eternally grateful to him for that.

I followed the men's suit-squared shoulders, and footsteps, a sound I'd learned in such a short time to come to dread, the sharp click of dress shoe heels on concrete. They were heading back in the direction of the office I had hidden in, rather than in the other direction, toward the medical bay. I wondered if Otto might be back down in medical. I experienced a spear of guilt at having cut him so badly.

I followed them down the corridor. We walked past the office where I'd found the phone, and I looked at the closed door longingly, wishing I could try to call my aunt again. But we kept going. Another, smaller corridor led off to the left, and we turned down it. It appeared to house only a single door at the end. I glanced back over my shoulder, toward the way we'd come. If we'd continued walking down that way, would we have come to an exit? Mentally, I pictured the layout of the building. Yes, I was sure it would lead onto the grounds at the back. My gut clenched with longing for my freedom, but I knew it wasn't going to happen. I could try to run now, but I wouldn't get anywhere. Both Stewart and Bryson had their weapons drawn in preparation for me trying something. They'd learned not to trust me now. Had Hollan heard about what Stewart had tried to do? If he had, he made no mention of it.

The door we'd stopped in front of was guarded by a code lock rather than a key. I watched as Hollan's fingers flew over the buttons.

Six, eight, four, one, one.

The numbers flashed up in my personal space around my head, all in the same positions I'd always seen them. I imprinted their order to memory in case I ever needed it again. I didn't know how the next few minutes were going to pan out, but I'd have remembered those numbers even without trying, anyway.

The keypad beeped, and the door clicked open. It was made of solid metal—thick and heavy. Hollan pulled it open fully to reveal the room behind.

My mouth dropped open. Like the door, this room was also lined in metal. I'd never seen the interior of a bank vault, but I imagined this was exactly how one would look.

We were standing in what appeared to be a giant safe.

The only difference was that this safe had furniture inside—a desk, a chair, and a computer. Small drawers with locks made up much of the walls, but I had no idea what was inside them. Did one of those little drawers contain the memory stick? I scoured the fronts of the drawers, as though something about one of them might be able to give up its secret, but they all looked exactly the same.

The walls were bulletproof, I realized. No one was getting in here without the code Hollan had just punched in. Isaac's instincts when he'd said Hollan wouldn't have just left the memory stick lying around were correct. He'd predicted we couldn't just kill Hollan because he would have kept the stick protected by a code of his own, and he'd been right.

Only I had that code now.

I could kill Hollan the first moment I got the chance. I just needed to get my eyes on that memory stick.

Adrenaline soared through my veins. I glanced between Stewart and Bryson. They were both armed, and I guessed Hollan still was, too—I remembered the gun in the holster, which he'd flashed at me in the back of the car. If I could get Hollan alone, I could go for the gun. But Hollan was a paranoid man. He'd gone to get the two other men before letting me out of the cell for this exact reason. Yes, I might be an unarmed woman on her own, but he'd seen what I'd done to Otto's face. He'd underestimated me, and he wouldn't be making that same mistake twice.

My gaze darted around the small metal room. Maybe the flash drive wasn't kept in one of those drawers. Perhaps that was a ruse. It could be in the desk, or was it somewhere else entirely—in a hidden panel in the wall, perhaps? After what I'd seen over the past week or so, nothing would surprise me at this stage. I stood, rooted to the spot, waiting for Hollan to make his next move and reveal the location to me. As soon as it was in my sights, I'd do whatever I could to kill the son of a bitch, even though I knew I was risking my own life as well.

Hollan took a couple of steps forward—

A blare of alarms sounded through the building.

W*haa-whaa-whaa-whaa* ...

The men all froze then looked to each other.

My emotions were mixed. A part of me thought, *shit, I almost had it,* while the other part wondered what the noise was all about. Did I dare hope the guys had finally arrived?

Hollan looked back toward the doorway, a frown pulling down his wide forehead. "Looks like we've got company."

He didn't need to tell the other two men what to do. They both backed out, and Hollan stepped toward the door, too. My stomach twisted in a knot, trying to think of a way I'd be able to stay, or get Hollan to reveal the location of the memory stick first, but he moved forward, the bulk of him forcing me to step back, too.

"We should stay in here," I blurted, shouting over the top of the alarms. "Show me the memory stick and I'll give you the code. We don't know what's going to happen now. This might be our last chance."

His eyes narrowed at me. "Why so keen?"

My cheeks burned. "Like I said, time might be running out."

"Whoever is out there isn't going to be getting in here. Even if they've brought a tank with them, they won't be getting through the entrance."

I thought to when I'd been outside, and how I'd considered there would be other entrances than the large one we'd entered via, which looked as though it was designed for vehicles. Could they get in one of the other doors? I didn't even know who was out there yet. I was hoping for the guys, of course I was, but I felt sure Hollan had plenty of enemies. It could be someone I'd never come across before.

"Come on." Hollan grabbed my arm and dragged me back out. "I'll be interested to see who our visitors are."

I looked longingly at the metal room as he pulled me from it then slammed the door shut again. The keypad beeped, though I barely heard it over the alarms. A light behind the pad flashed red to show it was armed. I knew the code to get in, however. Hollan had no idea how my mind worked with numbers. Maybe he'd thought having to remember the code for the memory stick was as much as my little female brain could handle. Yeah, I was thinking in sarcasm.

Even so, I was disappointed to have had the opportunity snatched from me at that moment. But if Isaac and the others were here, that would surely make up for it. Would Hollan take me back to the cell and lock me inside? But no, he kept hold of me and took me to the glass booth at the entrance, where security screens were lined up across the front. The metal roll-down door was right in front of us, and I stared at it in hope, praying they'd barge right through.

"What have we got?" Hollan asked the man in the glasses, who'd been manning the booth the whole time. I assumed he was also the one who'd sounded the alarms.

Nervously, the guy pushed his glasses higher up his nose. "We've got company. Five of them, I think. Looks like they're trying to surround the building."

I took the opportunity to sneak in a glance, and my heart lifted. It was them!

From several different angles, I could see the men sneaking toward the property. There was Kingsley—always hard to miss—and Alex. I spotted Lorcan, looking tough in his leather jacket and with a large gun held at his side. He had come, despite having been fighting an infection.

But something worried me. They all looked as though they were moving with military precision, sneaking up on what appeared to be a dilapidated building from the outside. I touched my fingers to the spot where the tracker was. It was getting sore now—like I had a deep spot under my skin—but compared to all the other aches and pains in my body, I had barely noticed it. It must be working, however. From the way they were moving, they knew I was in here. I'd never been so overjoyed to see a group of men in my life, but with my happiness also came fear. They weren't showing any signs that they knew they were being watched, and I was terrified Hollan would have a way of picking them off one by one.

Two other men—the same ones who'd been following in the second car when they'd taken me off the road—came running toward us. They had that definite timed footfall and stance of military men. "We have a breach in security, sir," one of them called.

Hollan nodded. "Take the rear of the building. Make sure they're not coming in through the back."

Both men jerked their heads in nods and turned to run back down the same corridor we'd just come from.

"Go up to the roof," Hollan instructed Stewart and Bryson. "You'll be able to take them out from there."

My worst fears. If Stewart and Bryson started shooting the guys from the roof, they wouldn't stand a chance.

"No, wait!" I cried, putting out my hands, but unsure of what I to do. It wasn't as though I could wrestle the men to the ground.

A roof exit also meant there was another way to get in. What did the guys have planned? They would have a plan. They would have already assessed this place and would be coming in with a coordinated attack.

I hoped they had that tank Hollan had mentioned.

My gaze scanned the glass booth Stewart and Bryson were now leaving. Was there a button I could hit that would open the door? If I was able to do something to help give the guys access to this place, it would make this whole thing a lot easier. In my mind's eye, I saw myself opening the door for them, and then being able to tell them where Hollan was keeping the memory stick. I imagined how proud they'd all be of me, how they'd see what I'd been through in order to make this happen, how they'd consider me to be a part of their team. But I didn't have time for girlish fantasies. Steward and Bryson had both already pulled their weapons.

"What do you want to do with her?" Stewart asked, jerking his chin at me. His muddy brown eyes never left my face, and it sent a chill through me. Would he be looking for a repeat performance of what he'd attempted to do to me in the cell? "Want me to lock her up again?"

Hollan's lips twisted, and his eyes darted between the scenes on the monitors, and back down the corridor, toward the cell.

He shook his head. "No, actually. I think I'd like her to see what happens to people who try to get one over on me."

My stomach flipped, and nausea rose inside me. Was he going to make me sit and watch as Stewart and Bryson picked the guys off one by one, shooting at them from the flat roof? The idea of watching each of them drop on screen filled me with horror. I hated being here. I needed to be able to do something to help, though I was clueless as to what.

"I assume we're shooting to kill?" Steward asked as he pushed past me. He shot me a look of triumph, and I glared back at him.

Hollan nodded. "Yes. I want to see every single of one them dead."

Ice solidified in my soul.

If I lost all of them, what would be the point in fighting?

Chapter Thirteen

Stewart and Bryson took off at a run, heading toward the stairs that would take them to the roof, I assumed. Both men held their guns at their sides, preparing to shoot Isaac and the others.

"Get in there," Hollan said, giving me a shove from behind to push me into the glass room containing all the security monitors. "Maybe we should take bets on how long it takes for my guys to put a bullet in each of yours."

"They're not that easy to kill," I growled. "You've tried it once before, remember?"

"That was different. Then we were on their territory. Now they're on mine."

He was right, and that realization caused dread to settle like a stone in my gut.

I glanced back at the screens. The men had separated, surrounding the building.

Could I scream and shout, run to the big roll-down door and bang my fists against it and yell my warning? But this place was supposed to be soundproof, and bulletproof, and the guys would never understand exactly what I was trying to tell them. To look up!

But if I could get onto the roof as well, they'd be able to hear me. My mind flicked over everything I'd seen since I'd been here. I'd watched the direction Stewart and Bryson had run—back down the other wing of the building, where the medical bay was located. There must be a door with a stairwell located behind it, as I hadn't seen any actual stairs. But first I needed to get away from Hollan.

Though I loved being able to see the guys again, I was terrified I'd hear shots and see one of them drop to the ground with a bullet hole in his head or chest. I needed to get out of here. I wasn't cuffed or tied up in any way. I just needed a distraction, or to slip past Hollan. Would the guy in glasses try to stop me as well? I didn't know. He didn't look like he'd be much of a threat, but these men were employed by Hollan for a reason, and I didn't want to underestimate anyone.

Time was running out.

On screen, I watched Isaac point to the building and gesture to get someone who was out of shot to move closer. I didn't want to lose sight of them, but the monitor was the object nearest to me.

Moving fast, I grabbed the monitor by its edges. I was conscious of my injured hand, but I couldn't let my fears of hurting myself again slow me down. Dislocated fingers could be fixed, but I wouldn't be able to do anything to bring any of the guys back if they were killed. Heaving with all of my strength, yanking the wires out at the back, I swung the monitor at Hollan. He gave a yell of shock and surprise, automatically lifting his hands to protect his face. He held his gun in one hand, and as the screen hit him, he released his hold on the weapon, and it went spinning to the floor. Glass smashed everywhere, tiny pieces raining down around us like confetti. The other man had cowered back, his arms up over his head to protect himself.

My gaze darted to the dropped gun. I didn't have much time. Hollan would recover quickly enough, and then my moment would be lost. Darting forward, I snatched up the gun, ignoring the splinters of glass that lay on top of it, jabbing into my already painful hand. I pushed away the pain—the tenderness of my dislocated fingers, and the sharp jabs of glass—and I ran, taking off in the direction I'd seen Stewart and Bryson go.

"Get her!" I heard Hollan yell from behind me. He was talking to the other man. But the guy in glasses didn't look as though he'd been brought in for his fighting ability, and I assumed he was here more for the tech side of things. He wasn't about to chase me around the building.

My fingers tightened around the grip of the gun I'd stolen from Hollan. I wished I'd been able to shoot him right then and there, but he still hadn't shown me the memory stick, and though he'd taken me to the reinforced room with the code on the door, he hadn't actually put it in front of my eyes. He might have been lying, for all I knew, and the memory stick wasn't there at all. Fucking thing. I wished it never existed, and all of this pain wouldn't have happened. But wishes meant nothing, and I had to deal with reality.

Ahead of me, a door stood open—a fire escape. I hadn't noticed the door before, but now it jutted into the corridor, it was obvious. I ran, terrified I'd be too late, and I'd hear shots sounding, but Stewart and Bryson must be waiting for the guys to creep close enough that they wouldn't miss, but also so the others wouldn't have a chance to run once the first shots had been fired.

More shouts of anger followed me. Hollan was coming after me. He wouldn't give me another chance after this. I had to make this work.

I sprinted up the concrete steps, taking them two at a time. A small building was positioned on the top of the roof, which housed the staircase, and the door to it stood open. Through the open doorway, I spotted Stewart and Bryson standing near the edge of the roof, their guns aimed as they watched the guys approach below. The guys were unknowingly being stalked from above.

Not caring for my own safety, I opened my mouth and yelled as loud as I could. "They're on the roof! Gunmen on the roof!"

Both men spun to me, eyes wide in surprise. I set my sights on Stewart first, my fury rising inside me like a wild animal. I lifted Hollan's gun and aimed it directly at him, anger curling my lip and making my gaze hard.

My finger squeezed the trigger, just as Stewart lifted his own weapon in return. I held his gaze, challenging him to do it. If he shot me, Hollan would kill him as well. They still didn't have the code.

All the things he'd done to me flashed through my mind, how he'd mashed my face against the floor, and had tried to pull down my jeans from behind. I thought of how he'd grabbed my breasts and pushed his hand between my thighs when he'd been patting me down on the road. I remembered how his hot breath had felt against my ear, the stench of the cigarette he'd just smoked, and the revulsion it had sent through me. Maybe I'd meant only to use the gun as a threat, but my body had other ideas.

I squeezed the trigger, the gun rocking in my grip. The crack of gunfire cut through the air, and a moment later Stewart took a staggered step back. He glanced down at the bullet hole in his chest, and the gun he held dropped from his fingers. He looked up at me in disbelief and his mouth opened, but no sound came out. His legs seemed to give way beneath him and he pitched backward, but he was too close to the edge of the roof. Almost comically, he slumped down on his butt, but he tilted back as he fell. His weight and momentum kept him going, and his legs flew up into the air as the rest of his body tipped off the edge of the roof. The last thing I saw were his feet vanishing as he fell off the side to the ground below.

I heard the thump and crunch as he hit the cracked concrete surrounding the building. Someone—one of the guys, I assumed—gave a yelp of surprise as the body struck the ground close by.

I stared in shocked horror. I had killed a man. Taken his life. Something inside me changed at that moment. I'd been pushed to prove what I was made of, and I'd shown I could kill when needed.

Suddenly something hit me from behind, pitching me forward. I still had the gun, but it spun uselessly from my fingers, skidding across the flat roof. I bucked and wriggled, trying to get the weight of the person on top of me—Hollan, I assumed—to shift.

The guys were all still surrounding the building. They were exposed and vulnerable out there. Yes, I'd taken one man down, but there were others, and they wouldn't go down without a fight. I needed for them to get in here, and seeing Stewart fall like that had given me an idea. I wasn't sure I'd pull it off, however. Hollan would be even more paranoid around me now. I'd already pushed my luck too many times. He must not have his handcuffs on him, like he did in the field, or I figured I'd already be restrained.

"Darcy?" I heard my name called, distant, and it sounded like Clay. My heart swelled with emotion. I wanted to be back with them so badly it hurt. Did they know I'd been the one to kill Stewart? I hoped they'd figure it out, so they could see I was fighting with them as well, and not being some little princess sitting around waiting to get rescued. As well as that, I was able to tell them I knew where Hollan was keeping the memory stick, even if I didn't yet know the exact location. I just needed to figure out how the hell to get them inside the building.

Chapter Fourteen

Hollan's weight lifted off me, but I wasn't going to go along sweetly. I allowed him to try to pull me up, but I kept my knees folded, so it was impossible for him to drag me to my feet. I was at groin height—something I wasn't exactly happy about. I'd already taken his gun, and now I sought something else. Knowing the guys needed to get into the building, and seeing Stewart go off the edge like that, had put an idea in my head.

I'd watched how we'd gotten into the building when we'd first arrived. Hollan had used a fob against a keypad, which he wore attached to his belt. I needed to go on the offensive, keep fighting, and get my hands on that fob.

Shouts came from below. "Darcy?" Kingsley's deep voice this time. "You okay, Darc?" came Alex's call.

They must be keeping themselves pressed up against the building to prevent Bryson, who was currently peering over the edge of the roof, his gun pointed downward, from shooting at them. I was surprised none of them had tried to shoot him yet, but maybe they were worried about trying something in case they hit me instead. Or maybe stepping away from the shelter of the building in order to take a shot would put them at more risk than was worth taking.

I couldn't answer them to let them know I was still alive. I was concentrating on one thing, sneaking a sideways glance to Hollan's belt as he continued to try to force me to stand. By remaining on my knees, he was hunched over, his head close to mine. The key fob flashed at me from beneath the bottom of his jacket.

With a roar, I suddenly shot to my feet. The top of my head smashed into his nose, and he gave a matching snarl, releasing me to clutch his hands to his face. His nose poured blood, and the tears caused by me hitting his nose so hard blinded him to my actions. I darted forward. With his hands at his face, his belt was exposed. I moved quickly, reaching in to snatch the fob off the leather.

Too late, he realized what was happening.

"Stop her!"

Bryson spun toward me, aiming his gun. Would he shoot me now? He'd watched me kill his friend. I saw him hesitate. Would his hatred, or possibly even fear of me, be stronger than his fear of Hollan if he killed the one person who had the information Hollan wanted?

The hesitation was enough. I'd never been much of a thrower, but I did my best over-arm and launched the fob in the direction I'd heard the guys' voices coming from. "It's the key!" I yelled.

"Fuck!"

That was Hollan's voice. He'd realized what I'd done.

"Get downstairs," he yelled to Bryson. "They'll be coming through the front."

Fierce elation powered through me. I'd done it. The guys were getting in here, and I could stop fighting and hand everything over to them. They'd take down Hollan, and I'd be able to tell them where I thought the memory stick was kept.

Seeing I was dealt with, Bryson lowered his weapon and ran for the stairs. I assumed he'd be heading to the front of the building to join his comrades in attempting to keep Isaac and the others from getting inside.

Something cold jabbed against the back of my neck. My heart struck up a whole new rhythm, beating so hard I could feel it hitting my ribcage.

"You busted my damned nose, you fucking bitch. You really are your father's daughter."

His words were muffled by his swollen nose and the blood most likely pouring down the back of his throat, but I knew it was Hollan. I knew something else as well, much to my dismay. I'd been so focused on getting the fob and throwing it to the guys, I'd forgotten about the gun I'd dropped. Hollan's gun. The one he'd reclaimed and was now pressing into the back of my neck.

Shit.

I froze, praying Isaac and the others would find their way up here soon. I heard the rumble of the shutters coming up, followed by instant gunfire, each crack making me flinch. It was the two guys Hollan had sent to the back of the building. The guy with the black glasses, who didn't look as though he was capable of fighting his way out of a paper bag, might have also joined them if he'd managed to put his hands on a weapon. Was Otto with them, too? Did he know the identity of the men attacking and their reasons for being here?

I hoped none of the bullets fired had hit any of the guys. I couldn't bear the thought of one of them dying. A piece of my heart would die with them.

The muzzle jammed harder against my flesh, and I knew I'd find a ringed bruise there if I lived long enough for it to form. "You have no idea how much I want to shoot you right now," Hollan snarled. "I've never known a little bitch to cause so much trouble."

I tried to remain calm, though my hands trembled. I wanted to tell him I'd never tell him the code to the memory stick, no matter what I'd made him believe earlier, but I managed to clamp my lips around my words. Letting my mouth run away with me now might well be signing my death warrant.

I just hoped the guys would deal with Hollan before he finally decided to kill me.

He gave me a shove from behind. "Move."

He was going to use me as both a shield and a threat, to prevent the guys from killing him. It didn't matter. Even if he made his getaway, we'd still know where he was keeping the memory stick, and then we'd just have to track him down later. I knew I sounded far too confident for a girl who had the muzzle of a gun pressed into the back of her neck, but I had faith in the others.

More gunfire came from below. Hollan shoved me forward again. I was frightened of what I'd find down there. Would Isaac have made it to the stairs yet? Or were they being held back by the other two men whose names I hadn't even learned?

We made our way down the stairs, Hollan pushing me from behind, seemingly not caring if I tripped and slid down the rest of the steps. The door at the bottom remained standing open, and I wondered what I would find on the other side. My heart galloped, my eyes widening with every gunshot.

He pushed me out of the door and into the corridor beyond, making sure that if any bullets were headed this way, it would be me they'd hit first. But the corridor was empty. More gunfire sounded from farther away, back toward the entrance.

"Move," Hollan said, giving me another push. I knew which way we were heading, though I didn't know what his thinking was behind it. Were we going back toward the metal room where the memory stick had been kept, or was he bypassing that altogether, and hoping to reach the rear exit?

But no, he wasn't going for the exit. Hollan turned down the smaller corridor on the left, and we were faced with the heavy metal door ahead of us that led to the vault-like room. It seemed to me that even though he was under attack, getting hold of the memory stick was still the most important thing to him.

A shout came from behind us. "Hollan, freeze!"

He spun, holding me in front of him like a human shield. I held back a sob of relief as I found myself face to face with the men who'd come here to save me. None of the guys looked hurt, and that was the most important thing. Isaac led the way, standing a fraction ahead of the others. His shoulders were back, his chin lifted. Even after a gunfight, he still appeared unruffled, barely a hair out of place or a wrinkle in his gray suit. Lorcan was right behind him, leather jacket in place, not appearing to be struggling with his shoulder. Kingsley's broad frame was at the back, Alex beside him, both of them of a similar height, Kingsley, dark and broad, and Alex, fair and slender. My heart tripped as I locked eyes with Clay's stormy gray gaze, and he held me in his focus, silently telling me how he was going to get me out of this. That we'd all be together again.

My eyes filled with tears, but still my gaze darted behind them. "There are other men here!" I tried to warn them. "Be careful!"

Alex shook his head. "It's okay. They're dead."

"All of them? The Swedish blond guy as well?"

Isaac frowned. "No, we didn't see anyone matching that description."

I was just relieved they were all right. Had Otto run, or had he already left before all of this started? I didn't blame him if he had. This had never really been his fight.

Isaac focused his attention on Hollan. "Hand the girl over, and we'll consider letting you live. There's no way out of this, Hollan. Most of your men are dead. The ones who aren't ran. This is over now."

Behind me, I felt the movement as Hollan shook his head. "No. I'm the one holding all the cards here. You need to turn the fuck around and walk away."

Kingsley growled. "Not happening."

Hollan moved closer to me, his body pressing into my back. The gun jabbed so hard against my neck that I winced in pain.

"Stop that, asshole," Clay demanded. "You're hurting her."

"Oh, I can do a lot worse."

I wished there was something more I could do, a way of helping the guys out. But I'd pushed Hollan so far, he was on the end of a very tight string that could snap any moment. If it did, I worried it would result in a bullet severing my spinal cord and punching through my throat. That wasn't an injury I'd come back from. Having a gun that could do that kind of damage had a way of focusing the mind to the very spot where the metal touched flesh. I was finding it hard to think of anything except what it would feel like if that gun went off.

"You need to let me walk out of here, or I will kill her, I swear I will."

I wanted to believe he wouldn't, as he still hadn't gotten the information he wanted out of me, but a man could only be pushed so far, and I'd done a lot of pushing over the past twenty-four hours. He might still want the code, but there was a chance his desire to see me dead would overcome that.

"You're not going to kill her." Lorcan's dark hazel eyes narrowed at him.

"You want to take that risk?"

Hollan grabbed hold of my wrist and yanked, forcing me to take a step back, away from the guys. The metal room where I believed Hollan was keeping the memory stick was directly behind us. I remembered its metal walls and door, how I'd thought to myself that it would be impenetrable.

"Shoot him," I pleaded with the guys. "I know where the memory stick is. We can get hold of it ourselves. We don't need him."

"We can't take the risk, Darcy. He could blow your fucking head off."

Yeah, I'm aware of that, I managed to resist saying.

They were putting my life above the importance of getting the memory stick back. I didn't think Devlin would be too happy about that.

Hollan gave me another jab with the gun. "You think you're going to win because there are more of you? Don't you think I'd be prepared for this kind of situation? Don't you think I'd have backup coming? I've just got to wait it out."

"We're not going to stand here pointing guns at each other until your backup shows up," Isaac said.

Hollan laughed. "No, of course not. I have a better idea." He reached out to where the code lock for the door was, and hit a button right above it. I couldn't see the smile on his face, but I heard it in his tone. "I'll let them deal with you first."

Something above our heads began to whirr. I glanced up. What looked like a shiny, silver, metal screen or wall was descending from the ceiling. My heart lurched. That thing would come down and shut us off from the guys. We'd be locked inside here until the backup showed up and took care of the guys. In the meantime, I'd still be Hollan's prisoner. When I'd first seen Isaac and the others, I'd thought my ordeal was over, but now it occurred to me that this might only be the start.

Wild-eyed, I shook my head with the tiniest of movements, still terrified of the gun pressed into the back of my skull. Maybe it would be better if he did shoot me. I'd rather be dead than stuck with Hollan.

I stared between the guys' faces, seeing their understanding of what was happening, their indecision about how to react. The silver wall was low now, almost halfway.

"No!" The cry came from Clay.

He sprang toward me, skidding sideways, feet first, beneath the descending wall. His feet caught Hollan's ankles, taking them out from under him. I tensed, waiting for the gun to blast a hole through my throat. Miraculously, it didn't, and Hollan swung the weapon. I was certain he was about to shoot Clay, but instead the gun collided with Clay's skull with a sickening crack. Because of the way Clay had come in, sliding beneath the wall, he'd automatically been lower than Hollan, giving Hollan the perfect striking angle. Clay was knocked sideways, but he threw himself back at Hollan, his shoulder connecting with Hollan's gut. The two men grappled, and I discovered I was free.

"Darcy, go!" Clay's shout to me, muffled. Blood streamed down the side of his head as he fought Hollan. I reached for him, but he shoved me, sending me spinning toward the still lowering wall.

The guys' hands grappled at me, fingers wrapping around my ankles and wrists. Then they were pulling me under, toward them. I managed to glance in horror back to where I'd left Clay and Hollan. Hollan lifted his weapon again, and brought it down on the back of Clay's head. The crack was even more horrifying than the first, and right before the wall finally hit the ground, Clay's legs slumped beneath him, and he collapsed to the floor.

Chapter Fifteen

"**N**o!" I cried, banging my fists against the metal wall that had appeared between us. The wall felt completely solid, as though it had always been there, and the room and men beyond had only been a figment of my imagination.

"Do something!" I spun to face Isaac. "Shoot a hole in it. There must be a way to get him out of there."

Isaac moved to the metal slab and ran his fingers down the edges where the metal met the wall, then kicked out at the bottom near the floor. He looked over his shoulder at me and shook his head. "It's like you'd find in a safe room. It'll be bulletproof. We're not getting in there."

"No!" I cried again, my throat tight and painful with unshed tears. I went to the wall and yelled against the metal. "We won't give up on you, Clay. We won't, I swear. You hear that, Hollan, you son of a bitch? We can wait you out, you know. What do you have in there to survive? We can beat you on this, I swear it." My rant left my throat feeling as though I'd swallowed glass.

Would Hollan kill Clay now? No, I hoped he'd keep him alive as a way to get me back. At that moment, I'd have happily given myself over in return for Clay. I never wanted this to happen. Clay had given himself up for me—had risked his life—and now he was the one in trouble. It didn't seem fair on any scale of the word.

I battered my fists against the metal, not even caring about my injured hand and the pain that sent splinters of glass piercing up through my hand and arm. No physical pain could ever match the emotional pain I felt at the thought of Hollan killing Clay. Clay was bigger than Hollan, and younger, but the way Hollan had hit the gun against Clay's head, and the way Clay had dropped like a mannequin, poured dread into my soul like liquid concrete.

A hand on my arm stopped me. I looked to find Kingsley right there, and I folded myself into his big body. His arms wrapped around me, and I breathed in the spicy scent of him, the familiarity calming me. Though it broke my heart to think of Clay, having the other four here with me again made me want to cry with relief. Kingsley dropped a kiss to the top of my head and squeezed me tight. Another hand touched on my shoulder, and I glanced over to see Lorcan gazing down at me in concern, his lips pressed together.

They couldn't tell me they were happy to have me back, not when Clay had been taken prisoner by Hollan, but I could see in their eyes that they cared. That they'd missed me.

"We have to get out of here," Isaac said. "You heard Hollan. He'll be calling for backup, if he hasn't already. We'll be surrounded and forced to fight our way out. We need to leave before they arrive."

"But what about Clay?" I couldn't stand the thought of leaving without him. There must be something else we were able to do.

A gun lay on the floor beside the guys' feet. Clay's gun.

I motioned to the discarded weapon. "Why didn't he take it with him? He could have shot Hollan and gotten out of there."

Isaac shook his head. "He wouldn't want to risk a shooting match, not with you in such close proximity. He knew if he fired, Hollan would fire back."

"But how was he going to defend himself? How did he plan on getting back out?"

The reason dawned on me and my jaw dropped.

"He didn't, did he? He was just planning on getting me released. He never thought about what would need to happen for him to get out of there safely as well."

"Clay cares about you. He wanted you safe. That was all that mattered."

Tears filled my eyes. "What about him being safe? That matters to me! Didn't he think about what I'd do with him in danger?" The image of the blood that had been pouring down the side of his head filled my mind. I saw how his legs had slumped, as though someone had cut all the tendons in his body. Hollan might not have shot him—yet—but he'd hurt him, and hurt him badly.

"Fuck!" My scream was filled with fury and heartbreak. "There must be a way into that goddamned room! There must be!" I threw myself back at the wall again, clawing at the edges, searching for any kind of weakness or movement, but it felt completely solid.

Isaac looked at me, and I saw a softness in his eyes. It was pity, and sadness. Like a parent breaking the news to a child that a much loved pet had died. "Do you know of any other way inside?"

I thought of the metal room and shook my head. I was breathing hard, my chest heaving. "No, but there must be. Surely Hollan wouldn't have locked himself in there without there being a way of getting out."

Lorcan pressed his lips together, shaking his head. "It's a panic room. He'll stay in there, with Clay, until help arrives."

I clamped my hand to my mouth. "Oh, God."

"Which is exactly why we can't hang around here," Isaac said. "We need to figure out what to do next."

"We're getting Clay out of there." A hint of panic and desperation made my voice too high. "That's what we're doing next."

Kingsley's big hand touched my elbow. "Yes, we are. But we need to be smart about it. Clay wouldn't want any of us to put ourselves in more danger for him, especially not you, Darcy. You know how he feels about you."

I didn't, not really, but I nodded anyway. I felt as though the energy had been sucked from my body, and I no longer had the ability to stand on my own. Kingsley's big arm wrapped around my waist and he held me up as I leaned into him.

The tears came, great wracking sobs of a combination of grief and relief that I was free. I lifted my hand to cover my face, ashamed of my emotions.

Alex caught my hand, pulling it away from my face. He inspected my bruised and swollen knuckles. "Hey, what happened to your hand?"

I choked back a sob, but my voice came out wobbly and hoarse with tears. I spoke each word with a hitching breath between. "Dislocated ... the ... fingers ... I think."

"Who put them back?"

"I did."

His eyebrows lifted, and he looked at me with something between being impressed and disbelieving. "Wow. That took some guts."

"It fucking hurt." I debated telling him how I'd imagined them all with me while I'd done it, how I'd followed his instructions, even though they'd only come from inside my head, and how Isaac had watched out, and Kingsley had kept me calm, and Clay and Lorcan had comforted me. But he'd have probably thought I was insane, and now wasn't the time, anyway.

"I bet," Alex replied, his blond eyebrows still lifted

"Not that it matters now." I shook my head. Nothing else mattered except getting Clay back.

Though I felt wretched, I allowed them to guide me back up the corridor, toward the front of the building. My stomach lurched as I spotted the shape of a body on the ground. The red hair and short, solid body identified the man as Bryson. He was lying face down, and a bloom of red spread out across the back of his shirt where several bullets had punched through his torso. I thought I should feel something about his death, but I didn't. I was numb inside. All my emotion was directed at the loss of Clay.

We stepped around the body and kept going.

We reached the area where the glass booth was located, and I drew to a halt. Two more bodies were sprawled across the concrete floor, both face down. I left Kingsley's side and approached the bodies. It was the two who Hollan had called for backup. Neither of them was Otto. The realization I'd been looking out for him punched me in the chest. I hadn't wanted to see him dead.

I didn't see the man who'd been manning the booth either.

"Two of the men I'd seen here are missing," I pointed out. "A skinny guy in glasses, and a fair-haired Swedish guy called Otto."

"The guy in the glasses ran," Lorcan said. "He didn't put up a fight, so I let him go. I didn't see any sign of the Swedish guy, though."

Isaac looked to the others. "We need to watch out for him."

"He might have just run," Alex suggested.

Isaac nodded. "Possibly, but even so, stay alert."

Every step that took me farther from Clay hurt my heart. I wanted to run back and throw myself up against the metal wall and give myself back in return, but I knew the guys would never let me, and Clay would probably kill me himself if I tried. But it still didn't sit right with me that Clay was in there. How would we get him back? Only by offering Hollan something he wanted, and I knew what that one something was.

"Hollan is keeping the memory stick in the same place he's locked himself and Clay into," I told Isaac, suddenly remembering I hadn't yet divulge this important piece of information.

That made Isaac stop. "It's in there? With Clay?"

I nodded. "I don't know exactly where, but it's not a big space. It's like a vault that's protected all the way around. Hollan was going to show me where he kept it when you guys showed up."

"Damn." His fingers went to his lips as he thought. "We need to get into that room."

Chapter Sixteen

The rolling shutters at the front of the building remained up, allowing us to see outside to the cracked concrete with the weeds pushing through, and the half fallen chain link fence. It was almost fully light now. Morning. I'd been kept at Hollan's mercy for almost a full twenty-four hours, and now Clay had taken my place. Every time I thought of it, something in my chest tightened, and I found it harder to breathe. We'd get him back, we had to, and then we needed to kill Hollan. I was sick of that man coming into my life and fucking everything up. He needed to be dead.

The vehicles I'd been brought here in remained parked in the same position as when I'd arrived. I hadn't seen Isaac's van—the one from the base, which I assumed he was still driving.

We stepped out into the bright sunlight. I squinted against the light, but as my eyes got used to it, I spotted a mound lying on the ground. It took a moment for my brain to piece together what I was seeing, but then the mound gave a groan, and my stomach turned in a slow flip. It was Stewart, and the son of a bitch was still alive.

Lorcan pulled his weapon and moved toward Stewart.

"He was as bad as Hollan," I blurted. "He tried to … you know … force himself."

Lorcan's head snapped to face me. "He tried to rape you?"

I couldn't meet Lorcan's eye, my cheeks burning with shame. I knew it hadn't been my fault, yet somehow I still felt sick and guilty about it, as though I could have done more to defend myself.

His eyes darkened with anger, and my stomach flipped. "Mother fucker."

Lorcan stalked toward Stewart crumpled on the ground and used his foot to give him a shove. He let out another groan and rolled to one side. I didn't know how he could still be alive after that fall and being shot, but he was. With a bitter stab of satisfaction, I noted how his leg was bent at a strange angle, and figured it was broken.

Karma was a bitch, all right.

A part of me wanted to take the gun from Lorcan and finish what I'd started, but the other part had been through enough. I wasn't sure I could stomach the thought of approaching a man I'd already shot once, and caused to fall off a roof, and put a second bullet in him when he had no way of defending himself. Stewart was a nasty piece of work, but that didn't mean I had to lose my own humanity.

But Lorcan didn't so much as glance back to me to check if it was what I wanted. Instead, he aimed his gun at Stewart's head. Even though I'd been expecting it, the blast of the gunshot made me jump. Stewart jerked, then fell still, all without saying a word.

Lorcan stayed leaning over him for a moment. He made a rasping noise in the back of his throat, then spat at the body. I felt the fury radiating off him, more anger than I'd felt toward Stewart myself. I didn't dare say a single word. This was a side of Lorcan I hadn't seen before. A cold and merciless side. One I was very glad was aligning with me and not against me. Was this the reason Lorcan had been given the job of weapons expert, or was it this facet of his personality that simply made him interested in guns?

Finally, he turned and made his way back to the group. A little of the darkness had faded from his eyes.

"Let's get out of here."

We kept moving, remaining alert that Otto might still be around, or that Hollan would have called for backup by now, though I figured reinforcements would take a lot longer to get here. We passed through the broken gate of the chain link fence, moving at a jog. Silent tears streamed down my face at having to leave Clay behind, but I told myself we'd come up with a plan. We wouldn't leave him there.

Even so, the image of how his body had slumped, a dead weight, after Hollan had hit him kept flashing in my mind. What if we left here, only to find Hollan had left with the memory stick when we got back, and Clay was already dead?

"We're not going far, Darcy." Isaac always had an uncanny way of picking my thoughts out of my head, and now was no exception. "Just back to the van. I've got my laptop there, and we can watch the place with the satellite feed. Hollan isn't going anywhere, and we'll know if new people are arriving before they get here."

I nodded, trying to convince myself that Isaac knew what he was doing. It didn't stop the hurt in my heart, however.

We passed through the gate, but instead of continuing along the road—which we must have driven down when I'd arrived, but I'd never seen due to being handcuffed in the trunk—Isaac stepped through a gap in the trees. The others followed, and so did I. Glancing down, I spotted tire marks through the mud. Kingsley must have noticed them as well, as he used his boot to scuff them as we walked, kicking fallen leaves over the tracks to hide them.

It felt wrong to ask about anything other than Clay, but I had to know.

"My aunt," I said. "Where is she?"

Isaac glanced over his shoulder as he answered me. "Back at base. We had to take her back there so she'd be safe."

"And she's okay?"

He nodded. "Worried about you, of course, and feeling guilty as hell, but otherwise she's all right. Now she knows you were telling the truth, and we're not the bad guys like she thought, she's warmed up a little. We left her with Devlin. The two of them appeared to be getting on well enough."

"Oh, yeah?"

He gave a short laugh. "Yeah, they were."

I guessed there wasn't a huge age difference between them. I'd figured Devlin to be in his mid-forties and Sarah was early fifties.

"When you didn't arrive for so long, I thought ... I thought maybe ..."

My voice broke, choking with tears. They seemed to come too easily at the moment. I'd never been much of a crier, but now they sprang to my eyes at the slightest thing.

"That we weren't coming?" Lorcan filled in gently. He was back to his quiet, sullen self, the anger I'd witness before having vanished as though it had never happened. I wondered if we should have moved Stewart's body—hidden it so if anyone else arrived, they wouldn't be immediately alerted that something was wrong. But then I reasoned that the only people coming were the ones Hollan had called, and they already knew there was trouble.

I sniffed and nodded. "I didn't want to think that, but it did cross my mind."

"I'm sorry, princess. We had to take your aunt back, and then we had a problem with the software for the tracker. It's new technology and had some bugs."

I swept my hand up to the spot behind my ear. I winced as I got my nails beneath the tiny tracker and pulled. It was exactly like I was digging a tick out from my skin. The tracker resisted for a moment, and then released with a small pop. I touched the area where it had been, and a small amount of blood came away on my fingertips. I held the tracker out to Isaac. "What do I do with this now?"

"Keep it," he said. "It still might come in handy sometime."

I hoped it wouldn't, though I slipped the tiny tracker into the pocket of my jeans. I never wanted to go through anything like the last twenty-four hours ever again in my life. I thought I'd suffer from reoccurring nightmares for years to come, and I already had the nightmares about my father's death to deal with.

Ahead, a dark shape was hidden behind the trees. I exhaled a sigh. We'd reached the van. Thank God.

Isaac unlocked the vehicle and went around to the passenger side. He pulled open the door, and climbed inside. Without another word, he snatched up his laptop from where it had been hidden beneath the seat, and opened the screen. His fingers flew over the keys, his eyes focused on the screen.

Kingsley yanked open the side of the van, pulling the sliding door across, revealing the interior. Lorcan climbed inside, vanishing into the back.

"Let me look at that hand," Alex offered, turning his attention to me.

"It's fine, honest." I curled the injured hand against my body protectively.

He shook his head and held his own hand out to me. "Don't be stupid. Let me look at it, and tell me where else you're hurt, too."

"Give the poor girl a minute." Lorcan navigated his way back out of the van, his arms full of something. I spotted what he had and had to stop myself from throwing myself at him. "I can't imagine she was treated too well in that place."

He looked to me. "You hungry, princess?" he asked, and handed me a bottle of water, and then a store-bought sandwich still wrapped in cellophane.

I nodded eagerly, accepting the food and water from him.

Alex exchanged a glance with Lorcan, which I read as 'I'm not happy about you interrupting, but you did the right thing,' then he took the bottle of water from me, cracked open the lid, and handed it back. I gulped the cool water down, spilling some down my chin, splashing onto my chest. I didn't care. All I'd had in the past twenty-four hours was the bottle Otto had sneaked into me, and I hadn't even drunk all of that, as I'd used some of it to wash his blood off my hands. Not for the first time, I wondered what had happened to him.

With my thirst quenched, I tore off the cellophane sandwich wrapper and ate ravenously, not caring if the guys thought I looked like a mess. I barely even recognized what I was eating—ham and Swiss cheese, if I had to take a guess—but I didn't care. Food was food, and I'd probably have eaten almost anything by that point. Dinner had been the macaroni and cheese, more than thirty-six hours ago. I saw the timeline of my past sweeping across my vision to my left. Each moment in recent time was marked out by whatever meals I'd eaten, and there were definitely far larger gaps than there should have been.

Alex and Lorcan watched me eat, matching expressions of part amusement, part concern on their faces.

"You got anything yet?" Kingsley called to Isaac in the front.

"Not yet. Give me a minute. I think the amount of tree coverage here is causing issues"

Kingsley nodded and pulled a cell phone from the inside pocket of his jacket. "I'll call base, let Devlin know what's going on. The signal might be better closer to the road."

"Yeah, you're probably right," Isaac said, jumping from the car, carrying his laptop with him. "I'll join you and see if it helps."

Both Isaac and Kingsley moved away, toward the line of trees surrounding us. As I watched, Kingsley pressed the cell phone to his ear.

Alex beckoned me. "Let me take a look at that hand now?"

I nodded. My stomach was full, even if my heart was empty. It was stupid not to let someone who was medically trained take a look at my injury. I didn't know what he could do to help all the way out here, but the hand didn't feel as bad as it had when the fingers were dislocated. Just bruised and swollen, though I did worry about them popping out of the joints again. There was the medical bay in the building we'd left, but I didn't think we'd be going back there to get me painkillers or a bandage. I'd long ago lost the makeshift bandage I'd created with the bottom of my t-shirt, but I had no idea where or at what point.

To my surprise, Alex leaned into the van and pulled out a green plastic box with a white cross on the front. "It isn't much," he said, apologetically, "but there will be something in here to help, just to tide us over until we get back to base."

"With Clay," I replied, staring into his blue eyes earnestly.

He nodded. "Yeah, with Clay."

I could see they were worried about Clay, too. They weren't like me, in that I made my feelings perfectly clear, but I saw it in the exchanged looks, the tightness around the lips, and the drawn down brows. Not that it was surprising they'd be worried about him. They'd grown up together, and Clay was like a brother to them all. If we lost him, I knew my grief would be unbearable, but it would be nothing compared to how the other guys would feel. They'd had him in their lives since they'd been children, and a hole that big could never be filled.

"Come on," he said. "Climb into the back of the van. You'll be more comfortable there, and we'll have a bit more room."

I did as he instructed, climbed into the van, and made my way over to the back seat, which ran the width of the vehicle. I sat down, and Alex sat beside me.

I held out my hand. With the utmost gentleness, he took it, examining my fingers. A frown pulled his eyebrows together as he turned my hand this way and that. Finally, he lifted my hand to his mouth and kissed my knuckles. "You did all the right things," he said, lowering my hand. "I'm pretty impressed you managed to get the joints to pop back in again, though. That kind of thing would be enough to bring a grown man to tears."

I nodded and bit my lower lip. "There may have been some tears," I admitted.

His mouth twisted. "Shit, Darc, I'm so sorry."

I shook my head. "None of it was your fault."

We smiled at each other for a moment, and then Alex turned his attention back to my hand. "The main thing we need to watch out for is those joints not popping out of place again. Once you've dislocated something, all those tendons around that joint have stretched, so it makes it far easier to dislocate again."

"Yeah, that's what I was worried about. I used a piece of my t-shirt to make my own bandage, but I lost it somewhere." I gestured to the torn bottom of my shirt and my exposed midriff.

"I can do a bit better than that." He smiled. "But I'm not going to complain about the torn t-shirt."

I used my good hand to smack him on the shoulder, and he protested, but with a good-natured laugh.

"Let's get you sorted, then."

He opened the small first aid box and pulled out bandages and a couple of foil packets of tablets. "Anti-inflammatory," he explained. "They'll help with the pain and the swelling. Take them first."

"Thanks."

Alex popped the tablets out of the foil packet into my palm, and I used some of the water remaining in one of the bottles to gulp them down. I tried not to think too hard about what I was doing. My throat always tried to close over when I was taking tablets, and then I'd end up with them as a pulpy, bitter mess all over my tongue.

With the tablets swallowed, Alex placed my hand on his knee, then looped the bandage beneath, securing my two dislocated fingers to the middle one, which had gone without injury. I caught myself looking at him while he worked, drinking in every detail—from the slight bump on the bridge of his nose, to the way his top lip was thinner than his bottom lip, to the faint cleft in his chin. All the guys sported a good twenty-four hours' worth of stubble, and Alex's had come in darker than the hair on his head, and I couldn't help wondering about the color of the rest of the hair on his body.

"There, you're all done."

He lifted his blue eyes to mine and caught me studying him. My cheeks flared hot as he gave me a smile, knowingly, as though he had read exactly what I was thinking. I remembered the night we'd spent together back at the house, how I'd been caught between awake and asleep, and wasn't sure if I'd dreamed getting up close and intimate with Alex. I'd woken with no panties on, and a part of me wondered if I'd removed them in my dreams, and had been dry humping the poor guy in his sleep. I was too mortified to mention the whole thing to him. I guessed I'd never know for sure.

"Thank you."

"We're really happy to have you back, Darc," he told me, one side of his lips lifting. I knew it was a bitter kind of happiness, though. They'd gotten me back, but they'd lost Clay. It wasn't an exchange any of us would have chosen—except maybe Clay himself.

"I'm happy to be back with you all, too." I returned the sad smile. "I just wish it was under different circumstances."

He lifted his hand and placed it to my cheek, studying me intently, leaning in a little closer. "We'll get him back again. I swear it."

I held his gaze. "And kill Hollan, too?"

"Absolutely."

His fingers pressed against my skin, and then we both leaned in, drawn together like magnets. My eyes slipped shut and his lips pressed against mine, soft and warm. Our mouths opened, tongues sneaking out to taste. The kiss was soft and gentle, finding each other. Alex pulled me in closer, lifting my bad hand to place it over his shoulder, out of the way, so it wouldn't get hurt.

He held me against him, his arm wrapped around my waist, as though he'd been waiting for this moment, and now didn't ever want to let go.

Chapter Seventeen

A lex was kissing me as though the only reason he'd been put on this planet was to taste my mouth.

His fingers pressed against my cheek, his tongue darting into my mouth to tangle with mine. I sensed a quiet passion within him, sensible, reserved Alex, who was always looking out for everyone else. He was the first of the guys I'd come into contact with, the one who'd first grabbed me, and who I'd kicked in return. That felt like a different person now. I remembered how I hated him, but now I couldn't see a single thing to dislike about this amazing man.

I became conscious of movement in the van, the bump of the vehicle as someone else climbed in to join us, but I was too involved in Alex's kiss to see who it was. Isaac had been busy working on the computer, and Kingsley had walked away to call what had happened back to base. That only left one other person.

I felt the depression of the seat as someone sat beside me. A second set of hands swept my hair from the back of my neck and placed a kiss right at the point where my neck met my shoulder. The kiss sent a shiver through me, and I gave a gasp of surprise.

Alex noticed, of course, and we broke the kiss. I glanced back to find Lorcan behind me. I was sandwich between the two guys on the back seat—like the ultimate teenage fantasy—Alex on my right, Lorcan on my left.

A silent exchange passed between Alex and Lorcan.

"I was just telling Darcy how happy we are to have her back," Alex said.

Lorcan nodded. "Yeah, we are. Nothing felt right without you being around."

My heart hitched. I'd felt exactly the same way when I'd been parted from them.

"I can't tell you how happy I am to be here with you."

Stupidly, tears threatened, but I didn't want that. I'd done enough crying for the moment, and I was sure I'd be in for plenty more tears if we didn't figure out a way to get Clay back, unharmed. But right now I only wanted to enjoy the sensation of being pressed in on both sides by two incredible, gorgeous men, who both seemed to care about me.

Lorcan touched my chin, twisting my face toward his, and gazed down at me with his hazel eyes. They seemed to change shades depending on his mood—growing darker with anger, and also, I discovered, with lust. He shifted closer, and I met his movement, turning to face him fully, though I didn't like how it created space between me and Alex. Not that Alex seemed to mind, as I felt him move up behind me as well.

Lorcan studied my face for a moment, silently asking me if this was okay. I tipped my face to his, and that was all the answer he needed. His mouth crushed to mine, stealing my breath, kissing me with a ferocity so opposite to how Alex had kissed me. He transported me back to the moment when he'd pulled me out of the hypnosis Kingsley had put me under, pushing me up against the wall, crushing me with his body and kissing me hard.

It was just me, Alex, and Lorcan in the back of the van, and yes, maybe we should have been doing something more productive, but this felt like their way of pulling me back into the fold.

Behind me, Alex had slipped one shoulder of my t-shirt down and was kissing my skin. His hand slid down the back of my jeans and my panties, and, even as I kissed Lorcan, he reached down lower, to graze his fingers down over my bottom and cup my pussy. I moaned as his fingers parted my folds from behind and pushed inside me.

"Oh, God," I gasped against Lorcan's mouth.

Alex kept kissing my neck even as his fingers moved deeper inside me, first one digit and then a second, scissoring inside me and stretching me open. Lorcan's hand slipped under my shirt, shoving my bra up to free both of my breasts. His touch was as rough as his kisses. His fingers pinched my nipple, twisting just enough to hurt and send sparks of insane arousal right down to where Alex's fingers continued to push inside me. I wanted to feel some pressure on my clit, greedily needing contact there, and I pushed up against Lorcan, wanting to climb onto his lap to have something to rub against.

The space inside the van was limited, but I could see where this was going, and I didn't want it to stop.

I didn't even care about getting caught. In fact, the thought excited me. I thought Kingsley and Isaac would be more likely to jump in and join us than they would tell us off.

Lorcan pulled me onto his lap, but edged in the seat so he was facing Alex. We were lucky that it was a long bench seat rather than individual ones, which would have been less comfortable.

But at the same time, we were all aware of what was going on, knowing we didn't have much time. It was a flurry of groping hands and hot breaths, moans filling the interior of the van.

Lorcan's kisses left my mouth, to travel down my jaw and throat, so I moved around and kissed Alex again. His tongue darted between my lips, and I noted how different each man tasted. They were such a contrast—Alex's blond, to Lorcan's dark hair. Alex's skin free from tattoos, where Lorcan was covered. And then there was me sandwiched in the middle, my skin unblemished from tattoos, but covered in bruises instead.

We couldn't end up completely naked—we didn't have the luxury of time for that, and we were still aware that we were parked in the middle of the woods, and there was a good chance we'd have to spring into action at any moment. That didn't stop us from continuing, however.

I fumbled with the belt buckle of Lorcan's jeans, wanting to free him. The ridge of his cock beneath his jeans was obvious, and my hunger for him grew.

I pressed my palm on the outside of his jeans, rubbing up and down his length. I stopped to try to undo his belt and buckle again, but I didn't have use of my other hand, and it wasn't easy to do. Lorcan helped me out, and I shifted back, pressing more into Alex to give Lorcan space. Alex didn't seem to mind, and he moved back as well, giving us all more space, even while his fingers were still inside me, making me heady with pleasure. Alex wrapped his other arm around my waist and pulled my bottom up, so I ended up on all fours on the seat, with Lorcan undoing his belt in front of me, and Alex still fingering me from behind.

Alex's fingers slipped from my body, and then both hands moved around the front of me to undo my jeans and pull them, together with my panties, down my thighs. Cold air hit my hot, wet pussy, and I shook out one leg, to remove my foot from the leg of my jeans, though I kept the other one on.

Alex's face pressed between my thighs, his hands spreading apart the cheeks of my bottom, and his mouth against my folds. He licked me open, and his tongue speared me. My back arched as heat spread through me.

In front of me, Lorcan had freed his cock, pulling down his jeans enough that they sat low on his hips, allowing his erection to spring up from the thatch of dark curls. My mouth watered for him, and the heady scent of his musk reached my nostrils. I wanted nothing more than to taste him, to feel him slipping across my tongue, and to lift my eyes to his and watch the pleasure in his gaze as I did so.

I lowered my mouth to his lap, which in turn raised my bottom higher for Alex. His tongue was working miracles, and I arched my back, pushing myself out toward him, wanting more. He must have gotten the message, as his mouth vanished from my pussy, and I felt the shift in his body as he repositioned himself.

In front of my face, Lorcan lifted his hips. I used my good hand to wrap around the base of his erection, squeezing him and sliding my fingers up and down a couple of times. Then, keeping my eyes lifted to his, watching him as he smoldered down at me, his lower lip slack with lust, I put out my tongue. Starting at the base, I licked him right where his dick joined his balls, up to his glans. He sucked in a breath as I swirled my tongue around the head and then licked back down again.

"Ah, fuck, princess," he growled. "You have a wicked tongue."

I gave him a wicked smile to match my wicked tongue, and kept going until he looked like he was going to go crazy with lust. Then I reached the top once more and slid my lips right down over the top of him, drawing him across my tongue and sinking as deep as I dared without triggering my gag reflex. His hands knotted in my hair, but he didn't push me deeper. It was more like he was using the touch to connect to me.

I sucked Lorcan's cock, the glans slipping across my tongue, followed by his hard length as I moved lower. I wanted to give him the best I could, to make him want me and no one else.

The familiar tear of a wrapper came from behind me—trust Alex to be prepared for this situation, even in the middle of everything else. At least he was being safe, not that I'd have expected anything less from him.

Even as I sucked on Lorcan, Alex moved to his knees behind me. The head of his cock pushed against my wet folds and he nudged his hips, pushing inside me.

I groaned around Lorcan's cock, and his fingers dug deeper into my hair, his blunt nails grazing against my scalp. "Ah, shit. That feels so good when you moan like that. The vibrations are intense."

"You want me to make her moan?" Alex asked.

I sensed Lorcan nod more than saw it. "Fuck, yeah."

That they were talking over the top of me somehow made me even hotter. Hell, this was the sexiest thing I'd ever done.

Alex pushed deeper inside me, stretching me open, filling me. He was a perfect size for me, big, but not as intimidating as Kingsley had been. When he was balls deep, he reached around my body and his fingers found my clit. I'd been desperate for someone to touch me there since this whole thing started, and the effect was instantaneous. I bucked at his touch, pushing myself harder onto his cock, my mouth sinking lower on Lorcan's length. I was impaled by them.

Alex pulled out and thrust again, all the while keeping up the small circles he was rubbing on my clit. I moaned again, and Lorcan groaned in response. His breath was ragged above me and I could feel his size swelling. Pre-cum leaked from the head, coating my tongue in its salty flavor. Alex's fingers of his other hand dug into my hip as he fucked me from behind—driving faster, harder, deeper with every stroke.

The pleasure that had held me in its grip ever since Alex had first kissed me began to build toward my release. I was almost there now, so close I could taste it. The muscles in my stomach and thighs were rigid with expectation, and even though I still had a dick in my mouth, all of my focus was on the tightness building at my core. I was starting to lose myself, my mind drawing inward, to the point where I no longer cared who was on the end of the two cocks penetrating me, only that I reached the point of release.

I forgot about Lorcan as I came, unable to keep him going as my orgasm pulsed through my body. I cried out, my head hung, my mind shattering into a million pieces. But even as the orgasm began to fade, I moved my attention back to him, knowing he needed to experience the same release. Alex had also paused behind me, allowing my body to recover from the violence of coming, but as my breathing began to slow, his movements quickened again. Now that I'd had my orgasm, he removed his fingers from my clit—it was too sensitive to touch right now, anyway—and both hands grabbed my hips, his thumbs digging into my ass cheeks. He fucked me hard, slamming into me, shoving me forward with every movement.

In my mouth, Lorcan swelled, and he came hard, hot streams of salty cum jetting down my throat, almost choking me. I took it well, swallowing what I could, only a little leaking from the corners of my mouth.

"Ah, fuck," Lorcan groaned, gripping my head tighter, thrusting down my throat once, twice more, each time allowing a little more cum to hit my palate.

Behind me, Alex swore as well as he came, holding himself deep as the final throes of his orgasm shuddered through his body.

We tumbled together in a mass of heavy breathing, sweaty bodies. I wished there was more time for us to just be together, but the others would be back soon. It wasn't that I was worried about them seeing us, more that I knew there was a chance they'd come back with information and we'd need to be on the move.

We separated enough to pull on our clothes, though we'd managed to remain as dressed as we'd been able to during sex. We exchanged suddenly shy, but happy glances, and both guys made an effort to plant a kiss on my shoulder or brush up against me.

I enjoyed what we'd done and hoped it would happen again sometime, though of course I wanted Clay to be safe first. In fact, adding Clay into the mix would have made the sex even better.

The guys made me feel cared for, desired, cherished. And most importantly, they made me feel as though I was bigger than just myself. Like I finally had a place in the world, and it was with them, by their sides.

Chapter Eighteen

The low murmur of voices and the cracking of twigs underfoot signaled the return of Isaac and Kingsley. We climbed out of the van to join them.

"How's your hand after that?" Alex asked me under his breath.

I lifted it to show that the bandage was still in place. "It's fine. I made sure I kept it out of the way." I couldn't help the smile tugging at my cheeks.

Lorcan handed me a bottle of water. "Thought you might appreciate this," he said with a cheeky wink.

I laughed, my cheeks heating. "Thanks." I took the bottle from him and placed the neck to my lips, taking some deep swigs of the water, washing the taste of salt from my tongue and throat.

They emerged from between the trees, Isaac still holding the laptop open, Kingsley with the cell phone in his hand. They didn't look as though they suspected anything had happened while they'd been gone, though I felt like the smell of sex lay heavy on the air. At least I'd been rumpled looking when they'd left, and I was equally rumpled when they returned. Not that I minded them knowing, of course, but it wasn't something I wanted to be announced when we had more important things to be thinking about.

"What's the plan?" Alex asked Isaac. "What did Devlin say?"

Kingsley cleared his throat before speaking. "He thinks we've got this handled. He's not sending anyone else out. He wants us to make sure we get the memory stick."

I didn't know how to feel about that. The guys were a capable team, so I could understand why Devlin would think they were more than able to handle things on their own. Despite this, a part of me had been hoping Kingsley and Isaac would come back with some miraculous way of saving Clay that Devlin was putting into place.

"Any sign of Hollan bringing in the forces?" Lorcan asked.

Isaac shook his head. "Not yet, but they will be. We might be able to use it as a way to get inside."

I frowned. "How?"

"Hollan can't stay in there forever. When his backup arrives, that will be his cue to get out of there."

Alex stepped in. "But if he's out of there, and free, he won't have any reason to keep Clay alive."

"Does he have any reason to keep Clay alive now?" I asked, though I wasn't sure I wanted to hear the answer. I couldn't stand the thought that we were already too late, and there was nothing more we could do.

Isaac nodded. "Yes, he does. He knows we're still out here and that we won't just leave. He'll want to use Clay as a human shield while he's trying to get out, but there's also a second reason."

"There is?" I tried not to feel too hopeful.

Isaac settled his green gaze on me. "Yes, you, Darcy. You still have what he wants."

I swallowed hard and nodded. "Then let me swap for Clay."

He folded his arms across his chest. "No. We'll be in exactly the same position as we were before. That's stupid."

"So arm me, and then send me in. I'll kill Hollan and free Clay."

"Hollan is trained. He's not going to just allow himself to be shot."

Anger built inside me, the relaxed pleasure I'd experienced from being with Alex and Lorcan evaporating. "Well, we have to do something! We can't just wait for Hollan to come out, especially not if he won't come out until he's surrounded by a team of armed men. How the hell are we supposed to get Clay released then?"

Kingsley stepped in, lifting his hand in a stop position to try to calm the situation. "Darcy, take a breath. Rushing into this hot-headed is only going to get us in trouble. We're miles from anywhere out here, and we don't know where Hollan will be getting backup from, but the nearest city is miles away. It's going to take them time to put a team together, and then drive out here."

Isaac nodded in agreement. "I'm not proposing we do nothing, but we needed to regroup, get ourselves stocked back up with ammo, and reassess the situation. Plus, you'd been hurt, and we needed to make sure you were okay, too, love. Clay would have wanted that."

The mention of his name kept conjuring tears. "Yes, I know that."

"We'll make sure we're back at the building before Hollan's team arrives," Isaac continued, his tone authoritative. "As far as I can tell, that is the only road in and out of here, so as long as we make sure we keep the area surrounded, they'll have no choice but to drive right into the middle of us. They'll be focused on getting Hollan out and protecting him, and we won't be able to do anything until we see Hollan emerge from the building. If we start on the attack too soon, it will just push him deeper inside when what we want is for him to be lured out. If he doesn't know we're there, even better."

"He has cameras everywhere," I said. "They're on every external part of the building. At the front of the building, just as you go inside, he had a glass room filled with screens."

Isaac frowned, thinking. "The part he locked himself into with Clay, did you see any screens in there?"

My lips twisted, my memory taking me back to what I'd seen. "There's a computer. I don't know if he's able to access the external cameras with it, but if I was a gambling person, I'd put some money on that he could."

Isaac nodded. "Okay, we need to stay hidden, then. Keep to the tree line. If Hollan has communication with whoever he's got coming for him, we don't want him to tell them he's seen us. We spread out, each of us armed, staying in the tree line, and as soon as Hollan comes out of there—sneaking out like the rat he is—then we go in."

"Are we shooting to kill?" Lorcan asked, his expression serious.

Isaac looked to me. "You know where the memory stick is?"

"Yeah, I think so. I haven't seen it directly, but he took me into that room to input the code. It must be in there somewhere, though he's more likely to have it on his person when he tries to leave. He won't leave it behind."

"I agree." He looked back to Lorcan. "Shoot to kill, if that's what it takes. But getting the memory stick is the most important thing."

Alarm jangled through me. "Isn't getting Clay back the most important thing?"

"Clay knows the risks."

His words were cold and settled over me like a blanket of snow, freezing me right down to my core. "Please, Isaac, we have to do everything we can."

"And we will, Darcy. Don't try to tell us how to do our jobs."

I slammed my lips shut, knowing nothing I would say would make any difference. I made a silent promise that I wouldn't let Clay down, however, whatever Isaac said.

"I want everyone to be ready." Isaac addressed us all. "Eat, and stay hydrated. Check your weapons and reload. We'll move out soon, to make sure we have plenty of time to get into place, and be ready for when they arrive."

Everyone nodded in agreement and set about doing as Isaac had instructed. Cellophane-covered sandwiches were passed around, together with fresh bottles of water. I didn't feel much like eating, having eaten the sandwich before, but I drank some more water and checked on my hand which Alex had bandaged. It didn't seem to be any worse after the activity in the back of the van.

Something caught my attention, and I frowned. The thrumming in the air was faint, but definitely there, and I exchanged a glance with

Alex, who stood beside me, making sure he heard it, too, and it wasn't my imagination. He frowned at me in return, and then looked in the direction of the sound. I didn't like it. What was it? Distant loggers using chainsaws? Vehicles coming?

No, it was something else, and the realization made my blood run cold.

Chapter Nineteen

In the distance came the hauntingly familiar thrum of helicopter blades. The sound caused every muscle in my body to tense, and I looked at Isaac. "It's a helicopter. Someone's coming."

I gazed up into the bright blue fall sky peeping through the branches of the trees, anxiously waiting for the aircraft to appear, though the sound was still faint, and I assumed it was still some distance away.

Isaac looked back at me, worry causing lines to cross his brow, his lips thinning. "Shit! Looks like they've sent a chopper to lift Hollan out of here."

We'd expected Hollan's backup to arrive by road. Using the chopper meant they'd arrived far quicker than we'd anticipated.

Lorcan rubbed his hand over his mouth. "How are we going to handle this? It's not as though we've got the firepower to take a chopper down from the air."

Isaac shook his head, but he was already moving, heading toward the van. "No. We'll have to wait until they've landed. Our plan still applies. They've arrived to take Hollan to safety, and he'll have to come out of the building to make it to the chopper. He has no choice, and when he does, we'll be waiting for him."

"He'll use Clay to protect himself," said Kingsley, breaking into a jog to join Isaac at the van. "How are we going to fight against men and a helicopter?"

Isaac glanced over his shoulder. "The helicopter itself can't hurt us. It's no different than them arriving in a car. They've just arrived faster, and it means we can't chase them if they get away."

"He's not going leave the memory stick behind," I said, "especially now that I know where it is. He'll have it on him when he tries to leave"

Alex spoke. "I still don't see how this is going to work. If Hollan has got Clay in front of him to protect him, and the chopper is going to land at any minute, how are we going to get to Clay and the memory stick without someone getting killed?"

Isaac glanced up at the sky. The noise of the helicopter was getting louder. "We'll surround the place. There are four of us, five if you include Darcy. And Clay isn't helpless either. Yes, he might have been unconscious when we last saw him, but that doesn't mean he's stayed that way. He might be able to fight back. We can take them from every angle."

Alex nodded in agreement. "Hollan will open the doors as soon as he sees the chopper land, and that will be our opportunity to stop him."

"I don't like this," I said, worry twisting through me like vines. "I can see Clay getting caught up in the gunfire if we start shooting at Hollan. Hollan's men are going to start shooting back."

Isaac shot me a look. "What else do you expect us to do, Darcy? Should we just let them walk away from this? The minute Hollan gets into the helicopter, he will shoot Clay dead. Do you understand?"

Ice pierced my heart at his words. I understood.

"We don't have any choice," Kingsley said. "I know this is hard for you, but sometimes we need to make these difficult decisions."

I blinked back tears. "I understand."

"Good. Then we need to move. We don't have much time."

The sound of the chopper had grown louder, the pulse of blades whacking through the air. If I never saw another helicopter, it would be too soon. How many men were likely to be on board—two? Four? Eight? I didn't even know how many a helicopter held. The fewer there were, the better. I hoped, considering how fast people were arriving to help Hollan, they wouldn't have had time to put together a big team.

They'd been sent to get Hollan out, not fight us. They didn't even know we were still here.

From the back of the van, Lorcan started handing out weapons. Each man was given a high powered semi-automatic. He handed me one of the smaller handguns. I knew it wasn't his way of insulting me. Lorcan knew that was the kind of gun I was used to handling. Now wasn't the time for bad shooting.

"Come on!" Isaac jerked his head back toward the road. "We need to move fast."

With each of us armed, we set off at a run, back through the trees and toward the building where I'd been held prisoner. My body ached as I jogged, all of the bruises and grazes I'd received over the past twenty-four hours hurting with every single step. My footfall jarred my bad fingers, but I ignored the pain and kept going. I just prayed we'd soon have Clay freed and the memory stick back in the rightful hands.

My breath rasped in and out of my lungs as I struggled to keep up with the guys. They never left me behind, however, one of them always staying behind me to cover my back while the others ran up ahead. Even on a rescue mission, they still cared about my welfare. I was pleased they hadn't made any noises about leaving me at the van. It would have been easy for them to say it would be safer for me, but they'd already witnessed everything I'd been through. They'd seen I was able to be one of them, to do everything it took to bring the mission to an end for us all.

My feet struck the road, and, with every step, the sound of the helicopter got louder.

"We need to move!" Isaac shouted. He ran up ahead, Kingsley's and Alex's long legs making them fast. Lorcan, still not fully recovered from his gunshot wound, stayed back with me, but even so, we increased our pace, knowing we needed to reach the building before the chopper landed. It was close now, so close. My heart felt like it was going to burst from my chest, and my breath whistled from my lungs in wheezing gasps. The muscles in my thighs burned. I didn't think we'd make it, and it seemed almost impossible that the people inside the helicopter wouldn't spot us from the air. Where would we even hide around the building? With its flat roof, there were no porches or open doorways to hide inside.

Isaac seemed to read my thoughts as we reached the end of the road and the clearing where the building was located. Everything looked exactly as we left it.

Isaac made a forward motion with his hand. "Get under the tree cover," he yelled at us. "The chopper won't see us from the sky from there."

Isaac motioned us forward. Kingsley headed in the opposite direction, circling the building clockwise, rather than the anti-clockwise way we were running. We split up, using the circle of trees surrounding the grounds to spread out. Lorcan and I ran around the perimeter, behind the building. I kept the gun held down at my side, but I was prepared to use it. Once the chopper had landed, they wouldn't be able to see us if we approached them from behind the building. I didn't know which door Hollan would emerge from, but I hoped he'd have Clay with him. If he didn't, I would jump to the conclusion that we were too late, and Clay was already dead.

I didn't want to think too hard on the possibility of that coming true. Not having Clay existing in this world made my soul want to wither and die. He was too bright a spark to suddenly no longer exist.

We didn't have much time. As soon as Holland opened the door, we needed to be in position.

Every muscle in my body begged me to stop and rest, but I forced myself on. Saving Clay's life was far more important than any discomfort I might suffer. He'd put himself in this position for me, and I wasn't going to let him die for it.

We stayed under the cover of the tree canopy, but the helicopter was ferociously loud now, hovering above. They were checking out the scene, perhaps trying to make sure the space available was big enough for them to land. I didn't doubt that whoever was inside the chopper would also be armed, and, if they spotted us, they wouldn't hesitate to start shooting. We were the enemy to them, the outlaws. Hollan was the good guy in their eyes, but I assumed they barely knew a fraction about the type of man he really was.

For a moment, I had the horrifying idea that they would land on the roof, and then Hollan would get a free run to his escape route, but the pilot must have decided it wasn't big enough to make a safe landing. The building on top of the roof which housed the stairs reduced the amount of space for the blades. There were also wires which traversed overhead, and would have been lethal to a helicopter trying to set down.

The wind caused by the blades of the aircraft as it began to descend sent leaves and other debris whipping from the ground, scattering around us. The branches of the trees bowed under the pressure of the air.

I lifted my arm to shield my face as the helicopter lowered onto the cracked concrete of the abandoned parking lot. I couldn't look away completely, however. We had to watch the doors. Lorcan and I were near the rear of the building, and I watched the smaller exits with intensity, willing them to open.

Come on, Hollan. Where are you, you son of a bitch?

The helicopter was on the ground now, mostly hidden from our view by the rear of the building. If Hollan was going to try for an escape route, it was going to be now. I held my breath in anticipation, my gaze scanning the place for any sign of movement. Which door would he leave by? The rear exit to the right of the building was the closest to where we'd left him, but leaving via the front would bring him closer to the helicopter and reduce the amount of time he was out in the open and vulnerable.

Time seemed to slow, everyone waiting for who would make the first move. Did the occupants of the chopper know we were here? Even if they hadn't spotted us, they might have something like heat sensors which would reveal our positions. Either way, I didn't think the occupants of the aircraft were leaving the shelter of its metal shell in order to extract Hollan themselves. They were waiting for him to go to them, and so reducing the danger they'd put themselves in.

The door at the rear of the building cracked open, and my heart lurched in my chest. Clay appeared in the space first, but he wasn't alone. Dribbles of blood had dried down the side of his head where he'd been hit, and his eyes looked vacant, the lids dropping shut even as he was forced out into fresh air. Hollan appeared directly behind him, and I noted how Clay dragged his feet as Hollan pushed him forward. Clay looked to be barely conscious, though he must be to keep himself upright. Hollan wasn't strong enough to hold a man of Clay's size up by himself, even though Hollan was bulky with middle-aged muscle.

Hollan paused in the doorway, looking left and right, checking to see if there was any reason not to make a run for the chopper. In his right hand, he held a gun, the barrel of which was pressed against Clay's bloodied head. I knew the weapon wasn't for Clay's benefit—he wasn't going to be fighting anyone soon. No, Hollan was doing exactly what Isaac had predicted and using Clay as a human shield against us.

Isaac's words rang in my head. They would let Clay die, if that was what it took to get the memory stick back. I cared about the memory stick, about the reasons Devlin needed it, but I didn't care enough to see Clay dead.

My heart pounded, my mouth running dry. My palm had grown sweaty around the grip of the gun I still held at my side. I knew this wasn't going to go down well with the others, but I had to do something. If I could get my hands on the memory stick myself, then Clay would survive.

Taking a deep breath, I sprang forward, into the open.

Lorcan hissed from behind me, "Darcy, no!"

I hurried in Hollan's direction and lifted the gun, pointing it at him. Hollan saw me coming, and his eyes widened in surprise. He'd never expected me to come back.

"Let Clay go!" I demanded. "It's me you want."

I sensed Lorcan moving up behind me. "What the fuck, Darcy?" he yelled. There was warning in his tone, and a question ... *what are you doing?*

I ignored him. "Let Clay go," I repeated, directed my words at Hollan, "and I'll give you the code." I had to shout to be heard over the noise of the blades of the chopper, trying to drown out my voice.

"We've been here before, Darcy," Hollan shouted back. "You're not going to give me that code."

"I will, I swear it. I was going to before the guys showed up, remember? We had a deal. You were going to let me see what was on the memory stick, and in return I was going to unlock it for you. That deal still stands."

His eyes darted around, knowing the helicopter was waiting, knowing he had backup, but obviously torn between taking the help and potentially losing his one chance at getting what he wanted.

At the front of the building, the others must have realized something was going on. I heard a shout, then someone fired a gun, the crack of the gunshot louder than the helicopter blades.

"We're running out of time," I yelled, taking a step forward, keeping my gun trained on Hollan, just in case he tried to do something stupid. "Release Clay, and I'll come with you instead. I'll unlock the damned memory stick, and we'll bring this thing to an end, once and for all."

I'd never seen Hollan look more uncomfortable, his gaze flicking back and forth between me and the direction of the helicopter, hesitating, unsure what to do. I didn't like this side of him, preferring the man who had it together. This man had the appearance of a trapped, injured animal. Unpredictable. I had no idea if he was going to run or attack.

Hollan tensed, but then took a step backward, toward the door. I realized he was going to retreat into the building.

"No, wait!" I shouted, throwing down the gun I'd been brandishing. I didn't want Clay to be taken back into the building alone, even if it meant taking me prisoner again as well. I couldn't leave Clay like that. Seeing the blood, and the way he didn't seem to be able to open his eyes properly, broke my heart. He'd done this for me, and now I'd sacrifice myself for him if I had to.

This was madness. Hollan was giving up his chance of escape, and I was giving up my freedom, but I didn't care. I ran toward the building, ignoring Lorcan shouting behind me. Maybe Hollan figured the helicopter would come back for him as soon as he had the code, or they would wait long enough for him to retrieve it. Perhaps that was exactly what would happen. I didn't know. All I knew was I needed to be with Clay, and I needed to reach the door before Hollan pulled it shut and locked us all out again.

Hollan vanished back inside the building, but he didn't close the door. I reached the entrance and threw myself inside. I turned back for a moment to find Lorcan right behind me. He didn't say a word, but spoke to me with his dark, hazel eyes, a pleading look that said, *don't do this.*

I grabbed the handle of the big metal door and mouthed *I'm sorry,* right before slamming it shut, encasing me inside the building.

Chapter Twenty

I knew the guys would be furious with me. Isaac, in particular, would be mad as hell when he learned what I'd done, but I didn't feel I had any choice. I couldn't let Clay be used as a human shield and risk him getting killed. And I couldn't allow Hollan to retreat inside the building with Clay either. Clay wasn't in any fit state to protect himself against Hollan, and I wasn't going to let him be at the other man's mercy. At least in here, I felt there was something I could do to try to protect him.

Hollan was already partway down the corridor, half dragging Clay with him. He turned right, vanishing down the small corridor where the vault-like room was located. With my heart pounding, I chased after them. Rounding the corner, I discovered the metal wall that had been lowered in order to seal Hollan inside the panic room, was no longer down. It meant the guys could storm the building from the front now, though they had armed men and a helicopter to get past.

"Hurry up," Hollan yelled, twisting his face to me, while he continued to move toward the metal room. "If we're going to do this, we do this now, or I'll shoot your friend in the fucking head, I swear I will."

I believed him.

I hurried after them. I didn't want to risk Hollan losing it completely and killing Clay. If Isaac and the others were able to deal with the men in the helicopter, then it would be us against Hollan, which was a match he was bound to lose. I just had to keep Clay alive long enough for Isaac and the others to take down the men in the chopper. I hoped that was a fight they'd win, because if they didn't, we'd be royally fucked. I'd have given the code to Hollan, and most likely Clay and I would end up dead anyway.

Mentally, I reassured myself that I was doing the right thing. If Hollan had taken him out in the open, I was sure Clay would have been shot, if not by Hollan himself, then by being caught in the crossfire. At least in here there was only one gun to be afraid of.

The door to the metal room stood open. That told me there was nothing inside left to protect, which meant Hollan had the memory stick on him. I wondered why we were going back if the memory stick wasn't there, but then I realized that was where the nearest computer was located.

I was right.

Hollan dumped a semi-conscious Clay into one of the chairs then hit the key to bring the computer to life. He reached inside his jacket pocket and pulled out the small, black, oblong device. The memory stick. My breath caught. That was it—the thing everyone was after, right in front of me. I suppressed the urge to lunge forward and snatch it out of his fingers.

Hollan jammed the device into the USB port of the computer, all the while keeping his gun trained on Clay's head. I willed the guys to get here, but they couldn't arrive yet. If they did, Hollan was sure to kill Clay.

A screen flashed up on the computer asking for a password. Flashing lines waited for me to enter the numbers that were now dancing in front of my face. The code.

Hollan jammed the gun back against Clay's head, and Clay gave a moan of distress. His blond hair, matted pink with blood, fell across his face. I was terrified to think Hollan might have caused him brain damage or something else permanent. It pained me to see him like this when he was normally so filled with life.

"Tell me the code, bitch," Hollan snarled, "and no goddamned games, or I'll shoot him in the fucking head. Is that what you want?"

I didn't like the look in Hollan's eyes—desperation—as though he'd been pushed one step too far. Could I risk it? If I gave him the code, and the guys got into the building, they'd be able to kill him. Then Hollan knowing the location of the other bases wouldn't be a problem for anyone.

With shaking hands, my fingers rested on the keyboard.

Sudden panic that I'd remembered the code wrong and was about to wipe the memory stick flashed through me. Cold sweat slicked my palms. Perhaps that would be the best thing to happen? But no, if I did, Hollan was sure to kill us both. My nerves made me lightheaded and dizzy. I had to concentrate.

The numbers for the code flashed up around me in order, and as I saw each one, I hit the corresponding key.

Four, nine, two, zero, six, three, seven, one, eight, five.

I entered the final number, and the screen changed. In front of me appeared six sets of coordinates, each one correlating to a different base. I knew one of them would match the base I'd been to, the same place Devlin and my aunt were at now, but I had no idea which one. I stared at each of the figures, trying to imprint them onto my brain. As I saw each set, they appeared around me, circling me like planets around a sun. I needed to be able to pick them out of the air the first moment it was required.

"Download them," Hollan commanded. He leaned past me and pushed a brand new memory stick into the computer's second USB drive. What he planned on doing dawned on me. He wanted to be able to access the coordinates whenever he could, and, unlike me, couldn't visualize numbers at will. So to prevent him needing to enter the code each time, he was simply creating a new memory stick that didn't have the same coding my father had installed on the original.

I glanced over at Clay, hoping he was coming around, and would be able to do something to help, but he still looked out of it. Hollan was also staying alert, keeping the gun pointed at Clay, while he glanced between Clay and the computer screen. He was keeping me busy at the computer, making sure both hands were occupied, while staying far away enough from me that I wouldn't be able to try to throw something at him and go for the gun.

Shit. I was running out of time.

"Now, upload the coordinates to the new memory stick," he instructed.

I debated telling him I didn't know how, but I knew he'd call out my bullshit. No one got to my age these days without knowing how to do something so simple on a computer.

My fingers ran across the keyboard, bringing up the files and folders I needed. I clicked the mouse, and hit save.

Dread had lodged like a stone in my gut. I couldn't let him get away with the new memory stick, but I didn't know what to do. The guys were all still outside, I assumed, so Hollan still needed to get past all of them in order to make it to the chopper and escape. Would he try to use Clay as a shield again, or could I at least hope that he'd leave Clay alone now that he had me?

"There." I straightened from the computer. "I've done it."

"Show me."

I clicked into the folder for the new memory stick, and opened up the file for the coordinates, proving I'd done everything correctly.

He nodded. "Good. Now shut it down properly, and hand me them both."

Though I hated myself for it, I did as he instructed, and removed first the new flash drive, and then the old one. Hollan held out his hand, and I dropped them both into his palm. My gaze darted to his gun, but he saw me and shook his head.

"Don't even think about it, young lady. Try anything, and I'll kill your friend in an instant."

I was lucky he hadn't killed Clay already. I figured the only reason he'd kept him alive was to get my corporation. I wouldn't have cared if

Hollan had been pointing that gun at me, but when he was pointing it at someone I cared about, that was a whole different story.

He slipped the new stick he'd created inside his pocket, then held out the one my father had died to protect. He dropped the original to the floor, and lifted his foot and crushed it beneath his shoe. The stick fractured into a hundred tiny pieces of plastic and metal.

Hollan gave a smile, victorious. "Not much point in keeping you alive now that I have this, huh?"

I stared at him in horror, trying to think of something I could do ... anything ... that would save our lives.

From out of nowhere, something crashed into Hollan.

At first I thought it was one of the guys finally here to help, but then I caught the flash of white blond hair, tan skin, a bandage taped across his face. Otto! The two men crashed to the floor, grappling for the weapon—Otto on top of Hollan. I was terrified the gun would go off, and though I should have tried to help Otto, my instincts caused me to cower away, out of the line of fire.

I hesitated, unsure what to do next. My mind was going three ways. Gun. Clay. Memory stick. Which one should I go for first? Still, the two men fought for the weapon. Otto was younger than Hollan, but didn't pack the bulk of muscle that Hollan did.

A gunshot went off, so loud it hurt my ears. I let out a scream and ducked, fear filling my soul. The last I'd seen, Hollan still had the gun, and I was certain I'd feel a bullet punching through my flesh at any moment. When none came, I risked glancing back to where I'd last seen Hollan. He was scrambling to his feet still holding the gun, while Otto was on the ground. Otto was still alive, his hand pressed against the spot right below his collarbone. He'd grown ashen beneath his tan, and his fair blue eyes had filled with pain and fear. They darted to me, and then back toward where Hollan was making a run for the door.

Shit.

Surely, my time was up. Hollan would turn and put a bullet in both me and Clay, and then do his best to get out of here.

Hollan hesitated at the open doorway, perhaps wondering if it was worth taking the time to finish the job on Otto, and then kill me and Clay, or if something else would be thrown in his way. I was certain I was going to get shot. Instead of shooting, he continued into the corridor beyond. I watched him pull a phone out of his pocket, and caught the words 'roof' and 'out of here' as he spoke into the cell.

My breath caught.

That was where he was going. He was heading to the roof. I didn't know what to do. I had two injured men here, and I was unarmed, but Hollan had the new memory stick. He was going to get away. Outside, I heard further gunfire. Isaac and the others were fighting a battle of their own. Had Lorcan managed to tell Isaac what I'd done yet? Did they even know I was inside here with Hollan? The people in the helicopter would be trying to take off, and as soon as they did, they'd have an advantage over the guys again. But it would take time to hover across the roof and pick Hollan up. Maybe that would be a weak point where the guys could bring the chopper down?

I paused, kneeling beside Otto. The amount of blood spreading out across the white of his shirt worried me. "I'll be back," I told him. "Keep your hand pressed to the wound."

Otto nodded. "Just go."

At least he was still able to speak—that was something. I didn't know what had brought about Otto's change of heart. After what I'd done to him, I wouldn't have blamed him if he'd let Hollan kill me. Hell, if someone had sliced open my face, I'd have probably helped. Had he been hiding out in the building this whole time, or had he somehow gotten past Isaac and the others and sneaked back inside? Either way, I was thankful. If he hadn't interrupted, both Clay and I would most likely be dead right now.

I glanced back to where Clay was slumped in the chair. His eyes were still shut, his chin on his chest, but his breathing appeared to be slow and even, and there was no sign of any more bleeding. I wanted to go to him, to touch his face and put my nose in his hair, and let him know I was there, but I didn't have time.

From outside, I heard more gunfire, and my stomach twisted. It didn't sound as though the guys were getting here any time soon.

I knew which direction Hollan had gone—toward the roof. He had the new memory stick on him, the one that was no longer encrypted. He could access the information anytime he wanted. The coordinates I'd seen flashed up in front of my vision, a series of numbers winking in and out of life like digits on a computer screen.

Hollan might have the coordinates, but I knew what they were, too.

Feeling wretched for abandoning both Clay and Hollan, I made up my mind and ran for the door. My feet skidded on the polished concrete floor as I raced for the stairs to the roof, wondering what the hell I was going to do when I got there. Unlike me, Hollan was still armed, but I needed to do something. I couldn't let him get away.

I reached the bottom of the stairs. The door stood open, but there was no sign of Hollan.

Taking the stairs two at a time, I reached the top and pushed open the door which led onto the roof. The helicopter had already managed to take off, and now hovered above us. The wind from the blade whipped the hair from my face. The noise was deafening. I spotted Hollan standing in the middle of the roof, looking up as something was lowered down to him. It was a rope with plastic straps at the bottom for Hollan to secure himself into while he was winched back up. He still held the gun in his hand, and I didn't dare try to approach him for fear of being shot. Only the noise and distraction of the helicopter had prevented him from noticing me so far.

Where were the others? I didn't know what had happened on the ground, if anyone had been hurt. I'd heard enough gunshots, and there were bound to be casualties.

The bottom of the rope reached Hollan, and he grabbed hold of it, lifting his legs to cling into the plastic part meant for seating.

"Stop!" I yelled in desperation. But it didn't mean a thing. I had no way of making him halt.

My shout had caused him to notice me, however. As he hung onto the rope with one hand, he aimed his weapon with the other and squeezed off a couple more shots, forcing me to dart back inside the small building that housed the staircase.

Impotent anger filled me. The son of a bitch was getting away, and there was nothing I could do about it. Further shots came from the ground, and I realized Isaac and the others were firing from below, trying to take him out and shoot at the helicopter out from the ground. Hollan was in a precarious position, dangling from a rope at the bottom of the helicopter, but even before he had managed to get into the aircraft, it was already lifting and taking Hollan out of range.

I stood, staring, as the helicopter rose higher and higher. I caught a glimpse of hands reaching down, helping pull Hollan him into the body of the aircraft, before the door was pulled shut behind him. They were too high up now to make out any faces or details that could be used later.

Feeling useless, I slumped to the roof of the building.

Fuck. I'd failed. Hollan had gotten away, and not only that, he had the locations of each of the bases where the guys were trained. I was furious with myself. I should have done more, made different choices, but then I remembered the reason I'd made those choices—Clay was downstairs, hurt but alive—and Otto was there, too, also badly injured, perhaps even dying.

I didn't have time to sit around feeling sorry for myself.

Not while people's lives hung in the balance.

Chapter Twenty-one

I forced myself back to my feet.

My entire body trembled, and I felt lightheaded, but I had to go and help the guys downstairs. I needed to explain to Isaac what had happened, and we'd need to tell Devlin. I dreaded that moment, but at least one good thing had come from this. Yes, Hollan might know where the bases were now, or at least he had the coordinates for them, but so did we. We weren't completely helpless, and we could warn the other bases that Hollan might be coming to try to take them down.

As I started down the stairs, my legs weak beneath me, a male voice came from the bottom. "Fucking hell, Darcy. Are you okay?"

It was Kingsley—I'd recognize that deep tone anywhere.

He came into view, and I spotted Alex close behind them. Guarding from the rear were Lorcan and Isaac. They must have seen Hollan leave, but didn't want to let their guard down in case more of his men remained in the building.

I nodded, trying not to cry. "He got away. I'm so sorry."

Alex's lips pinched as he looked at me, his gaze scanning my body. I knew he was looking for any further signs of injury. "It's okay. It doesn't matter. You're alive, and that's what counts."

"Clay and Otto need help."

Isaac frowned. "Who?"

"I'll explain later, but he's been shot." I set off at a run, back toward the metal room where I'd left the two injured men. The four guys followed.

145

"He helped me," I called over my shoulder. "I don't even know if he's still alive."

Alex ran by my side, knowing he was the most important when it came to saving someone's life. "It's okay," he said. "I'm on it."

We reached the metal room where I'd left Clay and Otto. Otto was slumped against the wall, no longer pressing his hand against the bullet hole. The blood had spread across the front of his shirt, and his eyes were shut. Clay was still in the chair, and he managed to lift his head a little as we entered, his blue eyes open, and I was thankful to see recognition that we were here glinting in them.

Glancing down, I spotted the broken pieces of metal and plastic that had once been the memory stick we'd all been searching for. I didn't want to have to explain what had happened to Isaac yet, however, and I used my foot to try to push them to one side, hoping no one would get suspicious and start asking questions. It would need to come out, but not right now. Right now I needed them to concentrate on helping Clay and Otto.

"Shit." Alex dropped down to a crouch beside Otto and pressed two fingers against the inside of Otto's wrist to feel for a pulse. He frowned as he concentrated then gave a small nod. "He's still alive, but he doesn't look good. He needs a hospital. The bullet has most likely caused internal injuries which are more than I can cope with on the road. I'll patch him up for now, but we need to get him to the nearest hospital, and fast."

I nodded. "Okay. Whatever we need to do." I looked to Clay, who still appeared dazed, but was at least conscious. "Clay needs your help, too."

Kingsley went to Clay, crouching beside him. "Hey, hero. How are you feeling?"

Clay managed to lift his head, but doing so made him wince. "Head … fucking … killing …" he managed to grate out.

"Yeah, I bet. Hollan gave you a decent whack. Good thing there's not too much brain in there to damage."

His good-natured teasing caused the faintest of smiles to touch Clay's lips, and I thought it was possibly the best thing I'd ever seen. Clay was still in there. He was going to be all right. But the effort of trying to stay awake and communicate must have been too much for him, as his eyes rolled again and his chin dropped back down.

Kingsley looked toward us. "I think we need to get out of here."

Alex went to move Otto, but Isaac lifted a hand, stopping him.

"Wait." Isaac's jaw was gritted as he stared at Otto. "Who is he, Darcy? One of Hollan's men?"

I shook my head. "No, not quite. He was brought in to help. That's all."

"Help?" Isaac frowned. "He was helping Hollan?"

My gut twisted as it dawned on me that Isaac would probably kill Otto if he found out he'd almost injected me with drugs. I didn't want that.

"Yes," I said carefully, "but he didn't know the full story." I looked back at Otto, to the cut I'd given him. I'd slashed his face in return for him attempting to inject me, but he'd also saved me on two occasions. Maybe he hadn't started off as one of the good guys, but I wasn't about to let him die.

"You know what I'm asking you, love," Isaac said, catching me in his green gaze. "Is this man even worth saving?"

I nodded. "Yes. He's worth saving."

That was all I needed to say. Isaac took me at my word. "Come on, then. There's a hospital about twenty miles from here." He looked to Alex. "Is he likely to make it?"

Alex's expression was pinched. "I can't promise anything." He focused his attention on me. "You know we can't stay with him at the hospital, right, Darc?"

I nodded. "Yeah, I know."

We would have needed to explain bringing in someone with a gunshot wound. While it pained me that we'd effectively be dumping and running, at least I knew Otto would be in good hands.

We helped both Otto and Clay outside. Kingsley and Alex carried Otto between them. Clay came back around and was able to stand. Isaac wedged his shoulder under his armpit and took most of his weight, while I supported the other side. Lorcan, with his own injured shoulder, wasn't able to help physically, but he went ahead, covering us with his weapon in case other members of Hollan's team decided to make a surprise appearance as we stepped outside.

The helicopter had disappeared now. I thought I could hear the faintest drone in the sky, but it could easily have been my ears playing tricks on me. They were still ringing from the gun going off so close to me in the metal room.

I had to tell Isaac that Hollan had made himself a new memory stick, one that wasn't encrypted, and the thought of doing so made me sick with nerves. He still didn't know Hollan had gotten away with what he wanted and could access the coordinates at any time. I knew I needed to tell him, but my focus was getting help for Otto and Clay. We needed to get away from this place. For all we knew, Hollan might be sending a new team in to put an end to us.

We could fit Otto in the van, but the vehicles Hollan had used were still right outside, and they were closer.

"Take one of the cars," Isaac instructed. "Darcy, you go with your friend, and take Alex with you. Lorcan, you drive. We'll follow directly behind in the van."

We nodded our agreement. Alex and Kingsley were both carrying Otto, and they changed direction to take him to the nearest car. Clay was able to stand, but his eyes still rolled and his body felt loose, as though someone had cut all the ligaments. Though I knew Otto was in worse shape, it still killed me to have to leave Clay's side.

"We'll take care of Clay," Isaac said.

Alex must have sensed my reluctance, too. "He'll be fine," he called over to me. "Just a bad concussion, I think. We can take him for scans as soon as we get back to base."

The guys got Otto onto the back seat of the car. Alex climbed in beside him to try to help where he could, and Lorcan got behind the wheel. I assumed they'd be able to hotwire the vehicle if they had to, but Lorcan started the engine, so he must have found the keys still in the ignition. I moved to climb in the other side, but before I got into the passenger seat, Isaac stopped me, his hand on my arm.

"What happened back there, Darcy? We couldn't get to you. You shut the rear door behind you, and it locked automatically. The people in the chopper were covering the front entrance, so we couldn't get in there without risking getting shot, though we tried. It wasn't until the chopper took off again that we were able to get access to the building."

Nerves tumbled through me as I remembered I still hadn't told him that Hollan had managed to get hold of the coordinates. I was dreading his reaction.

"I should never have shut the door. I wasn't thinking straight. I only knew I needed to stay with Clay." I bit my lower lip and took a breath, before blurting out the bad news. "Hollan got the coordinates."

His head snapped to me. "How?"

"I had to give him the code. I'm sorry. He was going to kill Clay. I had no choice."

"Fuck."

"He downloaded them onto a new memory stick—one that wasn't encoded—and then destroyed the original."

Isaac's hand locked into his hair as he shook his head in disbelief.

I put out my hand as though to steady him. "But I saw the coordinates, too. I know where they are. We might not have the original memory stick, but I can tell Devlin the locations of the other bases, and we can warn everyone about Hollan."

"I can't believe that man got away again," Kingsley said, his hands on his hips as he shook his head. "He's like a cat with nine lives."

Isaac's lips thinned. "There's nothing we can do about it now. At least you know the coordinates as well." He shot me a look. "You're not going to forget them, are you?

I shook my head. "No, I won't. I swear." Even as I said the words, the coordinates danced in front of my face, a series of numbers with multiple digits after the decimal point, showing a total of six variations. I didn't know how accurate the coordinates would be. Did they show the exact locations of the bases, or did they only drill as deep as the city or region they were hidden in?

Isaac sighed and rubbed his hand over his face. "At least with us also knowing the locations of the bases, we can prepare people for a possible attack. If Hollan had gotten away with the coordinates, leaving the other bases open to attack, and with us with no way of being able to warn them, things would be looking a whole lot worse right now."

I nodded, thankful Isaac was looking at the positive side of this. He was right, but that didn't stop me from feeling wretched about the whole thing. I wished I could have done more. He must have seen my thoughts flit across my face, and his lips quirked.

"Hey, love, don't beat yourself up for this. We don't always expect to get the perfect outcome, we just do our best. Okay? I'm not going to pretend I like your impulsiveness or your need to be so damned self-sacrificial, but I understand why you did it."

"We got Clay back," I said, my voice small.

Isaac gave a half smile and bobbed his head in a nod. "Yes, we did, and that was mainly down to you."

I took that to be as close to praise as Isaac was ever going to give. I wasn't sure I deserved it, anyway. Yes, Clay was alive, and so was I, and we were able to go back to Devlin with the locations of the other bases, but Hollan also having that information wasn't the ideal ending to all of this.

Alex leaned out of the open rear door of the car, where he sat with Otto lying across his lap and bloodied rags pressed against the wound in his chest. "We need to go if you want him to stand any chance of surviving."

I gave Isaac one final grateful smile then turned and ran back to the car. Lorcan sat behind the wheel with the engine running, ready to go. The moment I jumped into the passenger seat and slammed the door, he was pulling out of there, the wheels screeching against the cracked concrete.

We left my old prison behind us.

Chapter Twenty-two

Lorcan drove with one hand on the wheel, sitting back in the seat, but pushing the car at speed, looking every bit the bad boy racer. All the way out here, it wasn't as though we were likely to come across another vehicle. Running into wildlife was probably our most likely hazard.

I assumed he knew where he was going. He wasn't using a sat nav, or apps on his phone.

"How's Otto doing?" I asked Alex, turning in my seat to look at him.

Alex's lips thinned. "He's still with us, and the blood flow seems to have slowed, but that could just be because his heart isn't pumping as efficiently now."

That didn't sound good.

"Do you think he's going to make it?"

"Honestly, Darc. I have no idea. He's one lucky son of a bitch if he does."

"Drive faster, Lorcan," I said.

Lorcan glanced over at me. "I'm going as fast as I can."

I bit my lower lip. Otto had taken that bullet for me. I didn't want him to die, but I also didn't want to feel the weight of his death on my shoulders. It was a completely selfish thing to think, but I couldn't help it. It was just another thing I'd blame myself for.

In the wing mirror, I caught sight of the black van, following at speed to keep up with us. I hoped Clay was all right. Alex had said it was most likely a severe concussion that was affecting him so badly, but

I'd seen how hard Hollan had hit him with the gun. He might have a fractured skull, but we wouldn't know for sure until we got back to base and he was able to have a scan. I wondered if it would be better for us to take Clay into the same hospital where we planned to leave Otto, but I knew the others would never go for it. They stayed under the radar, and that included avoiding places like hospitals, where too many questions would be asked.

As we got closer to the city, traffic began to build and Lorcan was forced to slow. Getting the attention of the cops wasn't something we wanted either. None of us wanted to explain why we had a man dying from a gunshot wound in the back of the car.

Lorcan navigated the streets, his neck craned as he peered out of the windshield. "Keep your eyes open for any signs for the hospital."

I nodded and copied his stance, my gaze flicking over every street sign. I glanced behind us to see we'd lost the van containing Isaac, Clay, and Kingsley somewhere along the way. I said so to Lorcan.

"Don't worry," he replied. "We'll catch up with them. I expect Isaac won't have wanted the van linked to this vehicle if we're caught on any CCTV."

That made sense. We could get rid of this car, but we needed the van.

I spotted a familiar sign. "Look, there." I pointed to the sign for the hospital. "Take the next exit."

"Great."

Lorcan did as I instructed.

In the back seat, Otto began to make a strange sound each time he took a breath, a rattle that didn't sound good at all.

"We need to hurry, guys," Alex called from the back. "Sounds like he's got fluid on his lungs. He's not going to make it much longer without surgery."

I leaned forward in my seat, as though that could somehow make us go faster.

A tall, gray building with numerous windows across each floor appeared to our left.

"There," I said, pointing, as though any of the others were likely to miss it.

Lorcan pulled into the emergency bay. It was currently clear of any paramedics, and I spotted an empty wheelchair sitting outside the entrance.

"Go and get the wheelchair, Darc," Alex said. "We'll get your friend into it."

I threw open the car door and rushed out. I wished it was nighttime, so at least I'd have been covered by darkness. Doing this kind of thing in the middle of the day felt even more wrong, for some reason. As I was grabbing the chair, Alex and Lorcan both helped pull Otto out of the car. I made it back to them with the wheelchair, and they placed him in it as gently as they could.

"You're going to need to take him in on your own," Alex said. "You won't look as suspicious as if a group of guys turns up with him. Tell them you found him like this, and that you think his name is Otto, but that's it. Then when he's in good hands, say you left your purse in the car, and get the hell out of there. We'll be waiting right around the corner for you, okay?"

I took a deep breath and nodded. He was right, and I needed to do this, but I still felt nervous. I couldn't hesitate, however. Delaying because of my anxiety might cost Otto his life.

I felt horribly self-conscious as I grabbed the handles of the wheelchair and pushed Otto through the doors and into the building. The smell of the place hit me first—the over-exuberant smell of bleach and other cleaning products overlying the baser stink vomit, blood, and shit. The soles of my sneakers squeaked on the linoleum flooring as I tried to get traction to push the wheelchair along.

There were people everywhere—lined up at the reception desk, sitting on plastic chairs, hugging each other in corners. I felt as though everyone was staring at me, as though they knew I was involved in something I shouldn't be. Truth was, everyone *was* staring at me. After all, I had an unconscious man, covered in blood, in a wheelchair. My gaze darted around anxiously, and I spotted a nurse rushing toward me. She was a little older than me, in her early thirties, at a guess, with silky dark hair which was tied into a ponytail. I felt horrible handing Otto over to this well-meaning woman, but I didn't have any choice.

"He needs help," I cried. "I think he's been shot."

"What happened?" the nurse asked as she reached me. She bent to place her fingers against a spot on Otto's throat to feel for a pulse.

"I don't know. I found him like this."

She glanced up at me, her lips thinned, her nostrils flared. "You should have called the paramedics."

I bit my lower lip. "I thought it would be faster if I brought him myself."

"What's his name?"

"Otto, I think. I don't really know him. I'm sorry."

"Right." She gave me a quizzical look, and I knew she didn't completely believe my story. "Has he got any ID on him?"

"I'm not sure," I repeated. I felt horrible about leaving Otto, but I was desperate to get out of there. The nurse motioned one of the doctors.

"We need a crash cart," she yelled, and, to my relief, took control of the chair. Wheeling Otto away from me, I gave him a final glance, wishing there was more I could have done.

"I'm just going to get my purse from the car," I called after the nurse, though she wasn't even listening. I was relieved, in a way, and backed up, taking a few steps, before turning and hurrying out the same way I'd come in. I ignored all the strange glances, keeping my head down, my hair falling over my face. I hoped I wasn't going to appear on CCTV, wanted for questioning regarding a man with a gunshot wound, any time soon.

As soon as I was outside, I started to run. Lorcan waited in the car a little farther down the road, and I kept up my pace, running toward it, desperate to get out of there. I wondered what had happened to the van with Isaac, Clay, and Kingsley inside. I hoped we would reach the base without Clay getting any worse.

Lorcan must have seen me coming in the rear view mirror. He leaned across the passenger seat and threw open the door, ready for me to scramble in. My heart thumped, both from the adrenaline, and from running.

I threw myself in and pulled the door shut behind me. Lorcan had pulled away from the curb and was back on the road before I'd even had the chance to catch my breath.

"How did it go?" Alex leaned forward, into the gap between the seats. Otto's blood covered his hands and the front of his clothing. He did his best to wipe his palms clean on the front of his pants.

"As expected. No surprises. He's in good hands now, though I still feel bad for abandoning him."

Lorcan's tone grew hard. "He was working for Hollan, princess. Don't forget that."

Alex spoke from behind. "Lorcan is right. Your heart is too big, Darc. He was brought in to hurt you. You did everything you could for him, considering."

I nodded and sat back in my seat. I understood their point of view, but they hadn't been in that cell with me when Stewart had tried to attack me. At least Stewart was dead. Plenty of things had gone wrong in the past twenty-four hours, but that wasn't one of them. I'd shot the son of a bitch off a roof, and then Lorcan had finished the job for me. I thought I'd have been feeling even worse about all of this if Stewart had managed to walk away.

Lorcan glanced over at me as he drove, one hand on the wheel. "Isaac wants to meet us on the outskirts of town. We need to dump this car, just in case."

"In case it's got a tracker on it?" I asked.

"Yeah, or if it might be recognized. The license plates might get reported or something, if Hollan is watching out for us." He shrugged as he watched the road. "Either way, we're better off getting out of it."

He was right. I didn't want to be in something that belonged to Hollan, anyway.

From the back seat, Alex called Isaac on his cell. I could only hear half the conversation. "Yeah, we're heading that way now ... No, everything went fine ... We'll see you in five." He hung up.

I kept checking behind us, half expecting to see cop cars chasing us, demanding to know more about what had happened to Otto, but everything remained quiet. Lorcan navigated the streets, driving neither too fast nor too slow.

Eventually, we reached the place where we were due to meet the others. The van was already there, parked on the street, but I didn't see any sign of the guys. I hoped they'd be waiting inside.

Lorcan pulled over, and we climbed out of the car and ran to the van. The door slid open as we reached the vehicle, and we were greeted by hands pulling us inside.

I smiled, pleased to see Isaac and Kingsley again. I looked to Clay, and my heart lifted with relief as I saw his eyes were open, and he was looking directly at me. He caught my eye, and his cheeks tweaked in a smile.

I didn't waste any more time, and climbed over the seats to get to him. "Oh, thank God, you're awake."

He winced. "Yeah, but my head is fucking killing me."

My expression matched his, feeling his pain. "You got hit pretty hard."

"That son of a bitch."

I took his hand, big and warm, in mine. "Thank you, Clay. You're crazy and should never have done it, but I appreciate you putting yourself on the line for me like that."

He gave a half smile, but I could tell from his eyes that he was still in pain, and that hurt my heart. "Hey, you did the same thing for me, from what I hear."

I squeezed his fingers. "Yeah, we looked out for each other."

"Too damn right."

His eyes slipped shut again, and his head rested back against the seat.

Alex and Lorcan had joined us in the back, and Alex slid the door shut, encasing us inside the van. Isaac and Kingsley were both back in the front, Isaac behind the wheel.

Lorcan dangled the keys for the car we'd taken from his fingers. "No point in making it any easier for Hollan to move, if he somehow does find it."

Isaac glanced over his shoulder at him and grinned. "Good thinking."

Isaac pulled the car away from the curb, and we were on the road again, heading back toward base. It was going to be a good couple of hours of travel, but I didn't mind. I felt safe again, being with all of my guys, and, if it wasn't for Aunt Sarah, and knowing I needed to deliver the coordinates of the other bases to Devlin, I'd have quite happily spent the rest of my life just traveling around with them all.

Still holding Clay's hand. I allowed my eyes to slip shut, and finally get some rest.

Chapter Twenty-three

The change in motion of the van as it drew to a halt woke me from my doze.

I rubbed the heel of my hand over my eyes, trapping a yawn tight in my jaw, and then leaned forward to try to get an idea of where we were. Forests rose all around us, and a dirt track led up the hill. Broken, rusted pieces of machinery lay abandoned around the edges.

We were back where we'd taken the van from—how many days ago? I calculated in my head, and the events of the past few days appeared as a timeline in front of my eyes, heading toward my left and vanishing behind me. Two days ago? Was that how long it had been? It felt like a lifetime.

Isaac had parked the van in much the same spot we'd taken it from when we'd gone to look for my aunt.

My stomach churned with nerves at the thought of how Devlin would react to finding out Hollan had gotten hold of the coordinates. I hoped he'd take it the same way Isaac had, seeing the positive of what had happened, instead of focusing on the negative. But it was a lot to ask. The negative was huge, after all, and would have massive repercussions. If I'd managed to keep the coordinates from Hollan, this would be over now, and they wouldn't need to warn the other bases. Instead, Hollan getting away would have an effect like a line of playing cards lined up against each other, the first one toppled over.

I assumed Isaac had already told Devlin what had happened via the phone, so at least he would have had a couple of hours to let things sink in. Unless he'd spent the time getting madder, of course. It could have been worse. I could have not seen the coordinates, and Clay could be dead. At least I'd be able to give him the coordinates, too. That was something. Devlin would be able to link back up to each of the bases, and they could figure out what they needed to do to protect against a possible attack from Hollan.

"Isaac," I said, leaning forward in my seat before we climbed out. "How much does Devlin know?"

He looked to me, his head tilted to one side as he assessed me. I always felt as though he was seeing more of me than I was comfortable with. "All of it, Darcy. I didn't have any choice."

"No, I get that." I frowned. "How did he seem?"

"As you'd expect. He's not happy about Hollan, but he's pleased we're all still alive."

"And the coordinates?" I prompted.

"He's happy to have them back, too." Isaac paused, considering me again. "He's not going to punish you, or shout, if that's what you're worried about."

I shrugged. "Not worried, just anticipating what might come, that's all."

He gave me one of his rare smiles. "It'll be okay, Darcy. We're all here for you."

I returned his smile. "Thanks, Isaac."

He might act like the tough case in all of this, but deep down he cared about all of us, I could tell.

The thought of seeing my aunt again also strangely made me nervous. I wasn't sure how I felt. I should be mad at her for what she'd done, but I was perfectly aware I was capable of making plenty of my own mistakes and would want to be forgiven for them. I should treat her in the same way I hoped people would treat me.

Though I was a city girl at heart, something inside me relaxed as I climbed out of the van, my feet hitting the dirt, and fresh air filling my lungs. Trees rustled their leaves around us, and birds tweeted at each other. It was hard to believe there was a whole community of people living beneath us.

The guys jumped out around me. Kingsley and Alex helped Clay, one on either side of him, their arms around his waist and his arms slung around their necks. Alex, I assumed, had cleared the blood away from the side of Clay's head, and I was relieved to see he was looking even more coherent. Seeing him in the metal room, after Hollan had hit him, had terrified me. The possibility of him having brain damage had flitted through my mind, and the thought of losing outgoing, fun-loving Clay in such a way was more than I could bring myself to think about. It would have been hard enough losing him, but watching such a bright light be dimmed to only a fraction of the man he'd been before would have been tortuous for everyone involved.

Isaac looked around at us. "Everyone ready?"

"Sure." Kingsley nodded. "Devlin will see we did everything we could."

My heart pattered. Did everything we could, considering the circumstances? I was fully aware of how much I'd changed things by being involved, but it wasn't as though it was something I'd been able to help. Perhaps I should never have insisted on bringing my aunt here, but, if I hadn't, Hollan would have taken her anyway and forced my hand. I assumed she'd never told Hollan where this base was, or he'd have already sent people here. Not that it mattered now, anyway. This base would be one of the coordinates I now had stored in my head. Hollan would figure out that where we'd met him on the road had been near that particular set. He'd know we were here.

I didn't know how much time we had. Taking on a place like this would take coordination and time; it wouldn't be something he'd rush into. I figured we had days rather than hours, but we'd underestimated how quickly they'd be getting help to Hollan back at the building where he'd held me, too. I didn't want us to make the same mistake again. Devlin would know more. What would they do? Leave and find somewhere new to start again, or would they stay and fight?

I guessed I'd find out soon enough.

Together, we walked the same trail, through the gate with the sign warning trespassers to stay out, and up the hill and around the bend. The last time we'd been here, it had been Lorcan who was struggling, but this time Lorcan walked ahead. Now it was Clay who slowed us down—not that any of us minded. We'd all have done anything for Clay.

As we rounded the bend, the tall, rusted machinery loomed overhead. I knew the routine now, and with that familiarity came comfort, my nerves giving way to a determination to make Devlin see I'd had no choice in doing what I had. The first time I'd been here, I hadn't spotted any sign of what lay beneath ground, but now I could make out the flattened area where the elevator rose from to take us down to the base. In fact, the entire area beneath which the base was located was flatter than the rest of the topography, and there were no trees or pieces of machinery located on that patch.

This time, Isaac didn't need to do anything to call the elevator. Devlin was expecting us. Deep underground, a mechanical whirring started, and the car began to rise. I assumed they'd stepped up security at the base, not only since my aunt had left, but since they'd learned Hollan now had the coordinates. Would he try to take on this base first, knowing we were here? It felt as though we were both gambling with time. The longer he took to prepare to attack us, the longer we had to prepare for him to arrive.

The elevator and the portable shell that housed the contraption had now fully emerged from the ground. I swallowed hard, my pulse racing and my stomach twisting itself into knots. After everything I'd been through, facing Devlin shouldn't be the most frightening thing, but it was.

The reason for my anxiety suddenly dawned on me. I was worried he would get the coordinates and send me back home. I was back to that same old thing again—this deep rooted fear of not being good enough. I wanted more than anything to be accepted as one of the guys, but I wasn't sure I'd done enough to prove my worth. If only I'd managed to stop Hollan getting away, then maybe Devlin would have seen I was capable. But I'd failed at one major point, and I didn't think it would be enough. Had that been my drive all along? Had I told myself I was doing this in my father's name, or that I was doing it to save the lives of the other boys still training at all the bases across America, but my real reason was simply to prove I was worthy enough to remain a part of the guys' lives?

The doors slid open, and the others stepped forward, Kingsley and Alex still helping Clay. It would be a tight squeeze with all of us inside, but we'd managed before.

"You okay, Darc?" Alex asked me with a frown.

I realized I'd still been standing in the same spot while everyone else had stepped inside. Forcing a smile I said, "Yeah, fine."

I shook myself out of my stupor and walked forward to join the men. Isaac was at the panel to choose which level we ended up, and Lorcan was on the other side of Kingsley, Alex, and Clay. Isaac hit the button, and the doors slid shut, encasing us inside. I was hit with a sudden moment of claustrophobia, the memory of being trapped in the trunk of Hollan's car flooding over me. I took a deep breath to steady my nerves, and then we were heading down. Claustrophobia in a place like the base wouldn't be a good thing to have.

The doors opened to reveal a number of serious looking men waiting for us. Devlin was at their head, and I recognized a couple of the others from the short amount of time I'd spent here before. Behind them, the security screens were playing images. Previously, only one had shown the outside area where we'd caught the elevator down, but now six of the screens were dedicated to the area of forest around the base.

I saw the gate with the sign which we'd passed through, and the van we'd abandoned at the bottom of the hill. They were being more cautious now. They'd gone for god-knew how many years without needing to worry about their location being revealed, but now they'd needed to step things up by a substantial number of notches.

As he'd done before, Devlin stepped forward and shook Isaac's hand. "It's good to see you all alive."

Alex interrupted, not giving Devlin a chance to welcome each of them individually. "I'm sorry, but we need to get Clay down to medical. He's probably only suffering from a bad concussion, but he needs checking over."

Clay managed to lift his hand in a single wave. "Sorry ... missing out ... debrief." The words were an effort for him, and I wanted to rush to him, to try to help in some way, though I was completely out of my depth. He was with Alex, and Alex would know what to do. Clay managed a grin, even though he was clearly still in pain. I didn't feel I'd had the chance to thank him properly for what he'd done, but I figured he'd appreciate my thanks far more when he was feeling himself again.

Both Alex and Kingsley retreated into the elevator, leaving me with Isaac on one side, and Lorcan on the other. I appreciated having both guys with me. Isaac had reassured me that he'd have my back, and I hoped he'd stick by his word.

Isaac nodded. "Thank you, Devlin. It was a close call."

"So I understand." His gaze moved to me, and I tried not to shrink beneath it. I hated that he had this effect on me, as though he made me feel younger than I was—a child again in an adult's body. "I'm sorry Hollan got away."

My teeth dug into my lower lip, and I forced myself to hold his gaze, though my natural instinct was to drop it to the floor. "Me, too. I'm sorry I failed everyone."

His eyes narrowed. "You have the coordinates?"

"Yes. I saw them when I was downloading them to a second memory stick for Hollan." Admitting I'd done such a thing made me feel wretched, as though I'd betrayed them by doing so.

"Then it wasn't a total failure," he said, surprising me. "And it wasn't your job, either. You may not have returned with the memory stick, but you have the information the stick contained, so, as long as you remembered it correctly, that's as good as the original."

I allowed my heart to lift, and I nodded. "Yes, I've remembered it correctly. My synesthesia means I can see the coordinates just by thinking about them."

"You took some risks to get them." He held me in his gaze.

"I felt the risks were worth it."

"Making big decisions without first consulting with your team isn't something we look favorably upon here."

"But I'm not exactly considered a part of the team, am I?" Where was he going with this? "It's not as though I was trained here, like the others."

"You've got to quit with the self-sacrifice, Darcy. If you're going to get anywhere in this job, you need to learn how to hold back your emotions and make sensible decisions."

I frowned stubbornly. "My self-sacrifice saved Clay, didn't it? And you have the locations of the other bases, even if the memory stick no longer exists."

"Yes, we do, but so does Hollan."

"I know, and I'm sorry."

He lifted a hand to stop me. "This isn't all on you, Darcy. In fact, none of it should be on you." He looked to Isaac. "What happened out there?"

Isaac stood straighter, and his hands hooked each other behind his body, as though he was military. "He was ready for us. The building he was in was fortified. Darcy knew she had a way in because of the code, and she took it. She was brave, and maybe a little reckless, but if she hadn't been, Clay would be dead right now."

"If she hadn't handed herself over to Hollan in the first place, none of that would have happened."

"And we'd still be no closer to the memory stick, and her aunt would most likely be dead."

The mention of my aunt made me realize I hadn't seen her yet.

"Where is Sarah?" I asked, not wanting to interrupt, but needing to know.

"She's safe," Devlin said. "She's downstairs, in the living quarters. The boys—especially the younger ones—have enjoyed having a motherly figure around."

"Did she apologize for what she did?"

He nodded. "Many times over."

"Can I see her?"

"Yes, of course. But first we need one thing from you."

He didn't need to say it. The coordinates.

He lifted a pen and pad of paper and handed them to me. I didn't hesitate, writing each of the numbers down in the order I'd seen them. I finished my final scrawl on the paper and placed the pen down.

"What will happen now?" I asked.

"We'll need to send teams out to each of the locations the coordinates reveal, and hope we get there before Hollan sends his men in."

I wondered if one of those teams would be Isaac and the others, and what would happen to me when they left.

"Do you think we will?"

His lips thinned, his nostrils flaring. "I hope so."

"I think Hollan will come here first," I blurted. "He'll be able to work out that the place he picked me up is the closest to one set of the coordinates, and know this is the place we came from."

"Hollan has no need for you now," Devlin said. "He has everything he wants, so his focus will have moved away from you. He has no reason to target this base any more than the others."

I nodded, trying to accept what he was saying. After all, Devlin was the expert. But, deep down, I felt the history between me and Hollan ran deeper than just needing a code for the memory stick. It had gotten personal now—me against him—and I was sure if he had the choice of where to attack, he'd want to put an end to me first.

I didn't argue my case with Devlin, however. He hadn't been there. He didn't know how Hollan had looked at me—as though he hated me with every fiber of his soul. Yes, he might want to take the bases out to put an end to these undercover agents who were meddling in their corrupt and underhand ways, but he'd want to see me dead, too.

Nerves thrummed within me, and I turned and left Isaac and Lorcan to finish speaking with Devlin. I wanted to see my aunt.

I caught the elevator down to the next level, where the kitchen and dining hall were located. The doors opened, and I stepped out. A couple of boys were hanging around; they looked to be about ten years old. They grinned and nodded at me before hurrying away.

I found my aunt wiping down tables in the dining room. A couple of the younger boys were hanging around her, helping out, though I suspected it was more to be in her company than anything. Though they might not acknowledge it on an outward level, subconsciously they must miss having a female influence in their lives. I knew how it felt to grow up without a mother, and though my dad had been amazing, there had always been this hole inside of me that I felt sure a mother's love would have filled. Maybe, when I'd gotten older, I should have made more of an effort to find her, but I was a stubborn one. I was of the mind that she was the one who'd chosen to leave, why should I be the one to chase after her? After all, she'd known where we lived all this time, but she'd never sent so much as a birthday or Christmas card. She could be dead, for all I knew.

Yet the woman standing with her back to me now, laughing with boys she barely knew, had taken me on. An angry, grieving, resentful teenager who had done nothing but cause her problems over the years. But she hadn't turned her back on me. Even when she'd sneaked out of this place and gone to Hollan, she'd done it because she'd believed I was caught up in the wrong crowd. Yes, she'd made a mistake, but we'd all made mistakes.

One of the boys noticed me—a tall lad with skinny limbs and spiky blond hair—and nodded in my direction. My aunt glanced over her shoulder to see what he was gesturing at.

Her mouth dropped open. "Oh, my God, Darcy!"

I smiled. "Hi, Aunt Sarah."

The cloth she'd been holding fell from her fingers, and she took a couple of steps toward me, her arms out, but then stopped, as though suddenly remembering what had happened, and realizing I might not be quite so pleased to see her.

I wasn't going to punish her for what had happened, however. If Devlin could see fit to let her back into the base, even though she'd put them all in jeopardy, I wasn't going to hold what she'd done against her either.

"It's really good to see you," I said.

She clamped a hand to her mouth and made a choked sound. "I thought you might not make it back alive. I was so worried. Blaming myself ..."

I stepped forward, and we fell into each other's arms. I squeezed my aunt tight, feeling her angular frame shudder as I held her. A painful knot tightened at the base of my throat, and I struggled to swallow against it.

"I tried to call you from the place I was being held," I told her. "I left you a message."

"Hollan took my phone from me the moment he picked me up from the road. I'm so sorry, Darcy. I didn't have it to be able answer."

So I'd made that call while Hollan had my aunt's phone in his possession the whole time. Dark laughter that I'd actually called the man who'd been hunting me tried to burst from my chest, but I managed to keep it down. "It's okay, Aunt Sarah. Everyone is safe now."

She shook her head, still not letting it go. "I should have believed you. I should have trusted your judgment."

We pulled away so we could see into each other's faces. She wiped at the tears on her cheeks as though she was angry with them, as though she didn't deserve to cry.

"We both made mistakes," I told her. "We can start again now, okay?"

She sniffed again and nodded. "I'd like that. I know I need to stop thinking of you as a little girl. You're a woman now, and a fearless one, at that. I need to start giving you credit for everything you've been through."

I gave a small laugh. "I'm far from fearless. I'm scared most of the time."

She reached out and took my hand, squeezing my fingers tight. "But you don't let your fears stop you from doing anything, and that, Darcy Sullivan, makes you brave."

Chapter Twenty-four

Now that I'd made peace with my aunt, my heart pulled me toward the bottom level, where I'd find Clay. I still didn't feel as though I'd thanked him properly for what he'd done for me. I also wanted to re-assure myself that he was going to be all right, with no lasting damage from the hit Hollan had given him.

I told Sarah I'd catch up with her later, and left her to finish up the tables.

I headed back to the elevator, smiling at each young man I passed, recognizing most of them. These were the people I'd done everything for in the end. Yes, I might have been motivated by my love for the guys, but ultimately, these were the lives I wanted to save. They'd be the Isaacs, and Clays, and Lorcans of the future.

The elevator was free from anyone else as I caught it down to the medical bay. I felt self-conscious as I pushed through the doors that led through to the treatment beds. I spotted Clay right away. He was ly-ing on one of the cots and had his eyes closed. A fresh white bandage was wrapped around his head, covering most of his hair. It was strange to see him without his blond locks falling around his face. He looked younger, somehow. More vulnerable.

I saw Alex standing with his back to me, looking over a folder of notes. He wore his white coat again, his stethoscope hung around his neck.

I cleared my throat, and Alex looked over his shoulder at me with a smile.

"Hey," he said, "I thought I'd see you sooner rather than later."

"I couldn't stay away. I needed to know how he was doing." I jerked my head toward Clay, though we both already knew who I meant.

Alex turned fully to face me. "It's good news. There's no fracture showing on the scans, so it was just a bad concussion. I've given him some pain meds for the headache. As long as he doesn't keep hitting his head, he should be fine, though obviously we'll keep a close eye on him over the next few days."

I smiled. "That's good to hear, Alex. Thanks for everything you did for him, and for Otto, too. I don't know what we'd have done without you."

He shrugged and glanced away, but a pink flush touched his cheeks. "Only doing my job."

Movement in the corridor outside caught my attention, and I saw Kingsley, Isaac, and Lorcan walking toward us. I didn't know what Kingsley had been doing—perhaps he'd gone back up to finish his debrief with Devlin while I'd been talking to Sarah—but they were all together now and must have had the same idea as I did to come and check on Clay.

"Hey," Isaac said as he walked in. "We thought we'd find you here." He looked to Alex. "How's Clay?"

"Going to be just fine." Alex grinned, flashing his straight white teeth. "Going to take more than a couple of cracks to the skull to keep Clay down."

Clay's voice came from the bed. "You guys talking crap about me again?"

So happy to see him conscious, a burst of laughter escaped my lips. "Clay, you're awake!" I bounded over to the bed. He'd already started to sit up, and I slipped my arms around him and pressed my face to his chest.

He laughed and rubbed my back. "I might have to get hit on the head more often if this is the welcome I get when I wake up."

I squeezed him tighter, inhaling the scent of him, hearing his heartbeat, slow and steady. "I'll wake you up like this every day," I said. "You don't have to get hit on the head to make it happen."

There was so much I still didn't know about the guys—who they were, what their backgrounds were, how much they remembered of their families. I felt as though I'd barely brushed the surface with them, but I wanted to know. I wanted to know every little detail. I meant what I'd said to Clay, but I could have said the same thing to any one of the guys. I wanted to wake up every day being able to hold each and every one of them like this.

He squeezed me in return. "That's good to know, sugar."

Not knowing how much Clay had been aware of, Isaac filled him in on what had happened.

Clay's expression grew serious. "So, we've still got one hell of a fight ahead of us."

Isaac nodded slowly. "Yeah, I'm afraid so."

The door opened behind us, and everyone turned to see who the new arrival was.

My heart sank as I realized it was Devlin. Was this the part where he told me that my aunt and I had outstayed our welcome? I'd done everything I could, and they had what they needed now. My job was done. We'd be sent back home, and I'd be lucky if I ever saw the guys again.

Devlin looked between us. "Ah, good. I'm glad I caught you all together." His gaze flicked to Clay. "Good to see you looking better, too, Clay."

Clay gave a barely perceptible nod. I assumed it hurt him to move his head too much. "Thank you, sir."

We glanced at each other. Were the others thinking the same as I was?

Devlin cleared his throat. "The reason I wanted to catch you all together was because this affects each of you. I wanted to get your thoughts on it. This won't work if one person is unhappy with the situation. I've never brought someone in from the outside to become part of an already established team before. You've all grown up together, so you learn how each other works on an almost instinctive level. You're bonded from childhood. However, what I've seen over the last week has surprised me, and it's made me consider how we do things."

I still wasn't completely sure where he was going with this, but my stomach flipped in anticipation. A part of me didn't want to hear what he had to say, while the other part just wanted him to get on with it.

Devlin turned to me. "You have a skill, Darcy, and it isn't one that can be taught. I can't deny that what you're able to do has a place with us. I can also see how you've bonded with the other team members."

I frowned at him. Though my mind was already putting together what he meant, I didn't want to believe it was true until he'd put it fully out there. "What are you saying?"

The older man squared his shoulders and lifted his chin. "That we have a big battle ahead of us, and we could use someone like you. Admittedly, you have some sharp edges that need rounding off, but I think we can make this work."

The weight of my fear of rejection that I'd been carrying around lifted from me like a heavy fog from a headland on a sunny day. "You're asking me to stay?"

"Not only stay, but become an official member of Isaac's team." He turned to Isaac and bobbed his head at him. "Assuming everyone else in the team is agreed, of course."

I held my breath. Isaac and I hadn't always gotten on, and I was aware I'd become closer to the others than to him in the time we'd spent together. I hoped that would change, though, and I was sure it would, if he only gave me the chance.

A rare smile spread across Isaac's face, lighting his green eyes. He looked like a different man when he smiled—kinder, softer, gentler—and while the hard Isaac was sexy as hell, I liked the look of this version, too.

"We'd all be more than happy to have Darcy on the team," he said. "To be honest, she's felt like one of us almost from day one."

My face cracked into a grin, and I looked between each of the guys, wondering if any of them would disagree.

"Maybe you should take a vote," Devlin suggested.

Isaac shrugged. "Sure." He lifted his hand into the air. "It's already a yes from me."

Alex raised his hand. "Absolutely. I'd love to have Darcy on board."

"I'm going to say yes," Kingsley said, lifting his hand slowly, and nodding and grinning at me at the same time.

I almost burst with pride.

"Hell, yeah," Clay managed to croak from the bed.

Lorcan nodded, and then jabbed his hand into the air. "Abso-fuck-ing-lutely."

I had to resist rushing to each of them and kissing them in turn, though I figured that wouldn't look overly professional to the man watching over us.

"It's agreed, then," Devlin said.

Isaac looked to me, that same smile spread across his handsome face. "Welcome to the team, love."

<hr />

THE END

<hr />

LOVED WHAT YOU'VE READ? 'Merging Darkness', Book four of the Dark Codes series is out now!

And if you enjoyed this book, or any of the others in the series, I'd love it if you took a moment to write a quick review. It only needs to be a line or two, just saying what you did or didn't like. Getting reviews can make or break a series, and give the author a boost to write you more books! Thank you!

About the Author

Marissa Farrar has always been in love with being in love. But since she's been married for numerous years and has three young daughters, she's conducted her love affairs with multiple gorgeous men of the fictional persuasion.

The author of thirty novels, she has been a full time author for the last six years. She predominantly writes paranormal romance and urban fantasy, but has branched into contemporary fiction as well.

If you want to know more about Marissa, then please visit her website at www.marissa-farrar.blogspot.com. You can also find her at her facebook page, www.facebook.com/marissa.farrar.author or follow her on twitter @marissafarrar.

She loves to hear from readers and can be emailed at marissafarrar@hotmail.co.uk and to stay updated on all her new Reverse Harem books, just sign up to her newsletter! https://landing.mailerlite.com/webforms/landing/e2x3e1

Also by the Author

The Monster Trilogy:
Defaced
Denied
Delivered

The Spirit Shifters Series:
Autumn's Blood
Saving Autumn
Autumn Rising
Autumn's War
Avenging Autumn
Autumn's End

The Serenity Series:
Alone
Buried
Captured
Dominion
Endless

The Dhampyre Chronicles:
Twisted Dreams

Twisted Magic

The Flux Series
Flux
After Flux

The Blood Courtesans Vampire Romance:
Stolen

Contemporary Fiction Novels
The Second Chances
Dirty Shots
Cut Too Deep
Survivor
The Sound of Crickets

Dark Fantasy/horror novels:
Underlife
The Dark Road

Printed in Great Britain
by Amazon